BLAZE

ECW PRESS
TORONTO

DIETRICH KALTEIS
HOUSE OF BLAZES

ECW PRESS
TORONTO

Published by ECW Press
665 Gerrard Street East
Toronto, Ontario, Canada, M4M 1Y2
416-694-3348 / info@ecwpress.com

Get the
eBook free!*
*proof of purchase
required

This is a work of fiction. Names, characters,
places, and incidents either are the product of the
author's imagination or are used fictitiously, and
any resemblance to actual persons, living or dead,
business establishments, events, or locales is entirely
coincidental.

Cover design: David Gee
Cover image: © San Francisco History
Center, San Francisco Public Library
Map of San Francisco, pre-earthquake,
created 1905 by A.B. Candrian

Purchase the print edition
and receive the eBook free!
For details, go to ecwpress.com/eBook.

LIBRARY AND ARCHIVES CANADA CATALOGUING IN
PUBLICATION

Kalteis, Dietrich, author
House of blazes : a novel / Dietrich Kalteis.

ISSUED IN PRINT AND ELECTRONIC FORMATS.
ISBN 978-1-77041-286-6
ALSO ISSUED AS: 978-1-77090-909-0 (pdf);
978-1-77090-908-3 (epub)

I. TITLE.

PS8621.A474H68 2016   C813'.6
C2016-902376-1   C2016-902377-X

PRINTED AND BOUND IN CANADA
PRINTING: MARQUIS   5   4   3   2   1

The publication of *House of Blazes* has been generously supported by the Canada Council for the Arts,
which last year invested $153 million to bring the arts to Canadians throughout the country, and by the
Government of Canada through the Canada Book Fund. *Nous remercions le Conseil des arts du Canada de son
soutien. L'an dernier, le Conseil a investi 153 millions de dollars pour mettre de l'art dans la vie des Canadiennes et
des Canadiens de tout le pays. Ce livre est financé en partie par le gouvernement du Canada.* We also acknowledge
the support of the Ontario Arts Council (OAC), an agency of the Government of Ontario, which last year
funded 1,737 individual artists and 1,095 organizations in 223 communities across Ontario for a total of $52.1
million, and the contribution of the Government of Ontario through the Ontario Book Publishing Tax
Credit and the Ontario Media Development Corporation.

Ontario
Ontario Media Development
Corporation

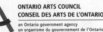

ONTARIO ARTS COUNCIL
CONSEIL DES ARTS DE L'ONTARIO
an Ontario government agency
un organisme du gouvernement de l'Ontario

Canada Council
for the Arts

Conseil des Arts
du Canada

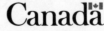

Canadä

RECYCLED
Paper made from
recycled material
FSC
www.fsc.org   FSC® C103567

TO ANDIE,
MY INSPIRATION

MONDAY, APRIL 16, 1906

. . . SLUMMER'S PARADISE

"I CAME back for what's mine," Levi Hayes said. "That and to kill a man."

Levi walked on, Mack Lewis looking at him, thinking he might have passed the man for a stranger a couple days back, the five years taking its toll; he'd always called him uncle, though first cousin once removed was closer to the mark. A flicker of lineage between them: the set of the jaw, the quick brown eyes, both men tall, the shoulders broad. But Levi's beard was showing grey, long hair going thin under the flat cap. Mack's hair pulled behind his ears, the bowler on top.

"See, to the decent folks, the Barbary's nothing but a back alley of vice and corruption," Levi said, looking at the old brothels up Whiting, mostly boarded up, waiting to be torn away. Ghosts from another time. "A moral cancer on this Paris of the Pacific."

"Learn that talk in prison?"

9

"Read it in the *Call*, talking about them and their cable cars and European opera and shit. How there's no place for all the debauchery and killing going on all the time."

"And you're figuring what's one more stiff?"

"Something like that." Levi grinned.

Mack guessing the only time his uncle spent on the Paris side was when he was robbing the rich. Just back from serving his stretch, nabbed when he couldn't explain the double eagle he laid down at the Ingleside track, trying to parlay his win from the first race on the nose of Black Cloud in the second.

The bet clerk possessing a sharp enough eye, noticing *In God we trust* missing from the face of the Liberty coin, a twenty dollar gold piece. The constable on duty clapping Levi in cuffs, same time Black Cloud finished in a dead heat.

The coin tied him to the inside job at the Old Granite Lady, the Mint down on Fifth. Levi shrugged when the presiding magistrate asked where he got the coin, not answering when asked about an inside man. The bang of the gavel sent Levi looking at a hard six in Quentin, less the twelve months for good behavior.

Sent up the same time the city blasted the hell out of Arch Rock out in the Bay, a menace to coast mariners, contractors drilling two hundred and sixty holes and packing in thirty tons of gelatin, blasting her skyward. The early edition declaring modern man now possessed the force of nature. Bottom of the page showed Levi's photo, the caption calling him a scoundrel, begging what happened to the missing thirty thousand in gold coins.

They passed the last of the dilapidated buildings on the block, all going to wrack and ruin. Properties Marvin Healey acquired for future expansion, keeping up with the shipbuilding going on over at Potrero Point. End of the row,

Levi stopped in front of a clapboard three-story suffering from long neglect, its paint peeling and faded, shingles missing, weeds waist-high out front. Looked like a good sneeze would take her to the ground.

Mack followed to the door, stepping over a board of nails. The sign hung above the door, red serifs long faded to brown, the gold outline flaked away: *House of Blazes*.

Snapping away a wood block holding the door closed, Levi shoved the door back on creaking hinges, walking into the dead air, a carpet of straw inside, dust playing in a shaft of daylight filtering down the stairs.

A line of ancient crates stamped with their ports of origin stood taller than a man along the west wall, boxes piled on the long bar. Casks and busted chairs clustered around a workbench, cobwebs hanging like streamers. Grime mossed everything colorless.

Mack held images of this place in its glory days, the long bar once packed with miners and sailors. Seen his own share of blind-drunk wrongdoing over at the Empress Dancehall, working as head bouncer. Nothing compared to this place and those times.

Pointing to where the Spanish chandelier once hung, big as a wagon wheel, Levi held out his arms, showing its size. Mack remembering.

"Had a gal early on called Hell Broke Lucy, wrapped to the eyes in a black rebozo, climbed up and swung from it, holding on with just her feet."

Hadn't heard this one, Mack let him tell it, always liked his uncle's stories. That look he got in his eyes.

"Pap's house rule was, any man climbing up to her got to go upstairs with her."

"Anybody do it?"

"You'd think with sailors working tall-sail ships, somebody would, but more than one got busted up in the fall."

"These fellows all drunk?"

"Pretty much." Getting the look of a man visiting his yesterdays, Levi stared to where the dance floor had been, the bar brought in from Placerville, the stairs leading to the boudoirs.

"Girls dancing atop the piano, lifting their skirts and flashing their wares." Levi pointing to where it stood. "Me, I'd be tickling the keys to 'Wearing of the Green' or 'Bird in a Gilded Cage.'"

Mack remembering him playing, wasn't too bad either. "Most folks learn piano playing in Sunday school." Then laughing.

"Learned mine from a bouncer, fellow named Nikko. When he wasn't busting up miners and sailors, he played a fine tune. Think he learned it at a proper school back east. Played till the brawling took toll on his hands. When he couldn't play or fight no more, Pap slapped an apron on him, made him bartender."

"Charitable."

"Didn't pay much, but the fellow had a way of adding to his per diem," Levi said. "Found himself a fish at the bar, the kind that wouldn't be missed so much. Served him drink laced with laudanum or some such." Levi went behind the bar, swatting away cobwebs, shoving boxes aside, saying, "When every eye turned to Lucy on the chandelier, old Nikko sapped the fish and . . ." Levi found the lever under the bar and tripped the trapdoor. It sprang open with a thump, right in front of the bar.

Mack stepped close and looked down the black hole, a dank smell coming up. "This Nikko do this regular?"

"Regular enough." Levi left it open, went and sat on a crate.

"Didn't learn that at no proper school back east," Mack said, sitting on a barrel.

"Not likely."

"What came of these fish?"

"Woke up on ships needing extra hands, mostly. Some captain willing to pay Nikko for recruiting them. Past that, I couldn't tell you."

"Jesus."

"Point is, this place rivaled the Bella Union, turned a fine trade before Marvin Healey found it a fitting place to stick his fucking shipyard."

They sat quiet, Levi with his memories, Mack looking around, hoping Levi was getting to why they'd come.

A rat scurried across the floor, Levi stomping his boot, sending it darting between the casks.

"Can't be thinking of turning this back to what it was?"

"Told you, came for what's mine." Levi pointed to the trapdoor.

"Gold from the Mint?"

Levi nodded.

"You hid it here?"

"Where'd you want me to put it, the bank?"

Mack never got to speak to Levi before the trial, couldn't during proceedings, and never went to see him in Quentin. Prisons giving him the shivers.

The Examiner reported that officials were befuddled as to how the thieves could have busted into the Mint and got thirty thousand in coins past the troop of guards. Marvin's brother Quinn, coming for Levi and making the arrest, searched the place top to bottom, but found nothing. Levi charged with the double eagle that was never issued. Flimsy evidence, but the Healeys saw that it stuck.

Rumor was Marvin Healey held sway with Meade, the magistrate presiding over Levi's trial, favoring the guilty verdict. A city official and golfing buddy had the property seized a week later, and Marvin bought it at auction for next to nothing. Land for future expansion of his shipyards. Marvin Healey known about town as a man of high integrity, a man who knew how to grease a palm.

"Chief difference between me and Healey," Levi said, "I do my robbing with a gun, that fucker does it with a pen."

"How in hell you get all that gold past all them guards?"

"Rats."

"Rats?"

"Dead ones. See, the Mint was infested to the roof beams. Started exterminating the vermin by the hundreds when I got this idea. Got myself chummy with the chief clerk, fellow name of Dimmick. A fellow with an equal taste for whiskey and women. So I poured enough in him, fixed him up with a fine gal, laid out my idea, and I had my inside man. Fifty/fifty. Dimmick stuffing rat carcasses with coins, right down the dead mouth. Six to a dozen, depending on the size of the rat, filled them like a sack, tossing them out a window, me waiting with a wheel barrow down in the alley. One or two busting open from the weight, but mostly they held up pretty fair."

"That's it?"

"Simple's best."

"And this Dimmick?"

"Being greedy on top of drunk did him in. Jury found him guilty on account of him forging the superintendent's name, stealing from pay packets and some other shit. Never could tie him to it, but they handed him a hard seven for the rest. Man's still in Quentin, drying his liver."

"And his share?"

Levi pointed to the trapdoor.

"Saving it for him?"

"Fuck him, he's a crook. You're a nephew. Giving it to you."

Mack lit up, standing, rubbing his hands, saying, "So what are we waiting on?" Going back to the trapdoor, looking down that hole.

"Didn't exactly leave it out in the open."

"So I'll go fetch picks, shovels, whatever we need."

"After."

"After what?"

"After I fetch back the deed."

"Don't need that. We'll dig nice and quiet, nobody the wiser."

"Healey fucked me once, not fucking me twice. Not going down there while his name's on the place."

"He just gonna hand it to you?"

"Uh huh. See, I got a plan."

Another rat zigged out, Levi thumping his boot, the rodent zagging across the floor, lost between the crates. "Turns out Marvin's missus likes the boys, likes them young and two at a time."

Mack raised an eyebrow.

"See, the woman comes by Pearly's Gates regular as a Sunday sermon. I'm guessing old Marvin's a man about town, but not in the bedroom, so his good woman figures he's not gonna miss a slice off a cut loaf."

"Yeah, but what's her getting her loaf cut —"

Levi raised a hand. "Had Pearly hire this photographer fellow . . ." Levi telling Mack they had to pay the man extra on account of Florence Healey being well-known for packing a derringer and rumored to suffer from vapors. The combination making the fellow nervous. But, for double his usual fee, he sat himself behind his tripod in the armoire in the boudoir, the door left ajar by an inch. The Healey woman liked to leave the lamps lit, adding to her visual delight.

"So, you're gonna blackmail her?"

"Not her, him. Get old Marvin to hand me five hundred for the rest of the photos, ones I didn't put in this envelope." Levi reaching in the inside pocket, showing the envelope. "Dropping it off at his shipyard when we leave. He pays or I go and besmirch his good name."

Mack grinned, thinking this could work.

"A lawyer draws up the papers," Levi said, "witnesses the deal nice and legal. Marvin gets his five hundred back, and I get the deed."

"So, you buy the place back with Healey's own money."

"That's the plan."

"Then you kill him."

Levi nodded.

Mack's grin faded. "Heard a couple of sailors tried robbing Healey of his watch and fob out front of the Bull Run one time, figuring him for a dude. Only one of them made it to Quinn's jail."

"I'll handle Marvin. Quinn, too."

"You got it all figured," Mack said, looking down the trapdoor again.

"Had five years for it."

. . . IN THE TRACES

BLOCK LETTERS ran up the chimney, the name rising high above the block-long structure: Healey Shipbuilding. Smoke from the stack rolled out over the Bay. A black gantry rose above the shipbuilding berths at the far end. A crane swung its load of iron above the roofline.

The sound of clanging metal came from within the compound, sparks flying as a crew welded steel plates to a hull. Silhouettes moved behind the rows of smeared windows facing East Street and the piers beyond.

A foreman waved in a steam locomotive hauling a low-loader piled with more of the giant plates, steel wheels trundling through Healey's gates, clattering over the criss-crossing tracks.

Levi and Mack stopped on the walk, Levi looking back like maybe they were being followed, waited till the loco-motive pulled into the yard. The foreman directed it to the plater's shack. Stacks of steel pipe and wagons being loaded with supplies. Across the street, the tenements afforded housing for the yard workers and their families. The bricks were all grey and the windows smeared. Children playing hoops and marbles on the opposite walk.

Going to the gatehouse, Levi handed the envelope to the watchman, was told Mr. Healey wasn't expected till end of day. Levi said that would be fine, asked the man to make sure he got it, slipping him a coin.

... LIGHTING THE FUSE

MACK STEPPED around a stubble-faced drunk, down on the sidewalk by steps leading to a basement dive, a sign calling the place Hevin and Hell. A flop hat tugged over the man's eyes, shutting out life, drool coming from his mouth.

"Locked me up with no proof," Levi said, "while fuckers like Handsome Gene run this town by hook or crook."

"Mostly crook," Mack said.

Back just two days and Levi was seeing the old Barbary disappearing like April ice, squeezed out by the progress of polite society. New corruption replacing the old. He could barely make out the top of Healey chimney above the Chicago Hotel now, shops on either side of it.

A line of men sat propped against the bricks of the Saint Anthony Mission. Loafers, low gamblers and jayhawkers the world forgot. Those conscious passed bottles and tobacco pouches, nobody paying these two outsiders much mind. Some talking. Some staring straight ahead. The Mission hadn't changed much, the white-paneled facade, name over the door, the gabled roof, the stained glass.

"So, you got out two weeks back," Mack said, wrapping his fingers round the cudgel in his pocket. "Working your plan."

"Stopped at the first bar I come to and got my fill of what they weren't serving in that shithole Quentin," Levi said.

"Built up a thirst, huh?"

"A powerful one." Levi grinned, taking in the line of men. "Met this gal Minnie Baker, girl from up Seattle way, something else they weren't serving. Took a room in some hotel, got a double helping, then we took in some auto race. Between her charms and my thirst, that woman had me heading north. Had me at the crossroads, forgetting my plan and going to work her daddy's sheep."

"Sheep?"

"Something wrong with sheep?"

"Smell, don't they?" Mack grinned, thinking his uncle had never worked a real job in his life.

"Woman claimed she got a bathtub right in her house. Running water and the whole bit."

"A woman of means."

"Trouble was, Minnie's love ran sober the night before the steamer headed north. Me, I woke up sick next to a note on the pillow. And my road was clear."

The woman likely pegged him for a con short on money and long on dreams, something Mack couldn't allow himself on account of relations, second cousin once removed. Mack thinking of that trapdoor and the thirty thousand in gold coins down that hole.

●

A WELL-TO-DO couple stepped through the Mission doors and down its steps, tailored clothes putting them at odds with the surroundings, likely there on some errand of charity. The man, in a homburg and frock, hooked his arm, the blonde wife slipping her gloved hand through his arm, escorted to their Runabout across the street, a Ransom Olds with the curved dash, artillery wheels and tiller steering, black-buttoned seats, the latest thing.

A grizzled warhorse sat propped against the front wheel, his head tipped down, a line of saliva dripping from his mouth. Talk and bottle-passing stopped, the men along the wall watching. The man roused, pushed himself up and tottered to his feet, looking at the woman in the Gibson-girl hat like he beheld the divine, steadying himself against the fender, then pushing off. His own forage cap, long faded, proclaimed him a veteran of the bygone war in the east. Something animal showing in his eyes, clouded by years of cheap drink.

Lurching into their path, he tipped the cap, drawling something neither made out, wiping the raisin skin at the back of his neck. Laying the hand on the woman's arm, he stopped her.

Delicate she may have been; still she ripped her arm away as if unclean were communicable by touch, raking the drunkard with indignation, her blue eyes flashing more anger than fear.

Warhorse laughed, regaining his balance like he was on a rolling deck, acting like he didn't see the husband, saying, "Like a gal's got fire, but you can lose the uppity, sis." Showing the backs of his hands, meaning he meant no menace. "I'm just making your acquaint-enance." Tobacco teeth behind the smile, he snatched her by the wrist, meaning to drag her over to the Mission wall, the woman trying to twist free.

"Here now," the husband said, "let go of my wife!" He caught her free wrist, tugging for the auto, grabbing hold of the door, the men along the wall hooting and rising, sensing amusement.

"You better than me, that it?" Warhorse let go, looking hard at the man, the husband stumbling into the fender.

"You want to make a play, fancy man." Warhorse showed the blade under the coat.

The derelicts at the wall egging him on.

"That'll be enough of this," the wife said, stepping between them, pointing a gloved finger. "I will call the authorities." The flush showing through the powder on her cheeks.

"She's got the spunk, boys," Warhorse called, snatching the wrist again and jerking her toward the wall, her hat falling. "Come and meet the fellows, sis."

"Let go." The husband summoned whatever resolve he could, catching her trailing arm, the two men pulling like it was a child's game of tug-of-war. "We got places to be."

"Then best get in your contraption, man. We'll send her along soon's we get ac—"

It was a good-sized stone that caromed off his head, the hollow thump of a struck melon. All eyes following the stone skipping past the Mission steps.

"Jee-sus Kee-rist." Whirling and clapping a hand to his head, Warhorse found himself facing Levi Hayes. His palm streaked with blood, fingering the rising lump, backing a step, sizing up the man: not some dandy, not drunk and not the law. Tall, lean and grey, the look of a man who didn't skirt around trouble.

"Best bring more than a fancy suit next time you stroll

the Barbary," Mack told the husband, bending for the woman's hat, brushing it off and handing it to her, tipping his bowler to her.

A look of thanks, the woman held the hat, let her husband help her up onto the seat. Quick getting in the Runabout, the man cranked the starter, retarding the spark, engaging the transmission with the shifter. Hand on the tiller, he sped off, the wife looking back, a smile of thanks.

"How much you think a thing like that sets a man back?" Levi asked Mack, meaning the auto.

"Couldn't say," Mack said, looking from the woman to the men along the wall. Most on their feet now, one urinating into the street.

Levi stood waiting, letting Warhorse think it through and call it.

"Buy a vet'ran a whiskey, and we'll let bygones go on by." Warhorse held his reb's cap out, smiling and rubbing the rising lump on his head, blood showing through his fingers.

"Veteran of what?" Levi flipped a second stone away into the street.

Stiffening to full height, Warhorse threw a salute, nearly losing his footing. "Gave them blue bellies what-for and bloody hell, right to the bitter end." Gesturing along the wall. "Most us boys did."

Getting some grunts and nods.

"Smells like you been pissing in that hat." Levi turned back down Battery and started walking, Mack eager to get out of there.

"Hey, how about that drink?" Warhorse called.

The drunks looking on.

"Won't drink with a man who'd piss on a cap of the Confederacy."

All eyes on Warhorse. A big man stepped from the wall, blocking Levi's way. Pickled in cheap booze, a milky eye, big-boned and well-muscled from a lifetime of working the sailing ships, saying, "You gonna let this fucker talk to you that way, Purvis?"

"No, I ain't, Hawk." Purvis stepped around Levi, facing him.

The line of men sensed more sport, one passing a grimy bottle, Purvis slapping on his cap, taking a drink, pulling back his buckskin to show the skinning knife, which looked like it had never been wiped clean. Feeling the upper hand now, he left the younger one to Hawk, holding the bottle out to Levi, saying, "Drink up, som'bitch."

Levi glanced at Mack, Purvis watching the exchange, missed seeing the fist that knocked him down, the bottle shattering, booze spilling on the walk.

Drawing the knife, he hissed and got back to his feet, blood dripping from his nose. The world spinning, two Levis in front of him. Licking at the blood, sweeping the blade at the one on the left, he stepped in and caught another fist. Going down again. Shaking his head, feeling like he just got punched sober.

Helping him up, the one called Hawk moved to flank Levi, forgetting about Mack, Mack cracking his cudgel across his skull, dropping the big man to a knee, the second blow laying him out. Mack turned to the wall, saying, "Anyone else?"

Dodging Purvis's blade, Levi clamped down on the man's wrist, upsetting his balance, sending an elbow into the bristled chin, the knife clattering down, the man reeling back, eyes wide, his arms whirling.

More blades and knuckles were pulled from pockets

along the wall, an empty bottle dashed against the bricks. Nobody feeling the ground shake under their feet.

Mack and Levi moved into the street, standing back to back, the men coming off the wall, forming a circle.

"Got any ideas?" Mack asked.

"You any good at running?"

"What's this, then?" The voice got heads turning, the circle breaking, men easing back to the wall, weapons slipping into pockets, some tossed down. The policeman stepped over the piss staining the walk, brass buttons polished, tall hat squared on his head. Hooking his thumbs in his belt, the pistol in an open holster, a billy stick on his belt. Looking at the line of men, then at Levi and Mack, back to Levi, amusement in his eyes.

"We was just having a drink and passing the time, Officer Healey," Purvis said, helping Hawk up, wiping blood from his face.

Hearing the name got Levi taking another look. There he was: Quinn Healey, the copper who'd dragged him to the courthouse five years back, cuffed him to the cell bars and beat him with his stick, brother of the man he'd come to kill.

The drunks backed to the wall. Whatever menace they had was gone. Quinn Healey stepped close to Levi, remembering, smiling. "Let you out, huh?"

"Good behavior."

"See you learned something about right from wrong."

"Funny, a Healey talking about right and wrong."

Quinn grinned, saying, "You still packing that old business?" One hand on his sidearm, the other on the stick.

"Not packing any business at all." Levi flapped his jacket back, showing he was unarmed.

"We thank you for stepping in, Officer," Mack said. "Now if you'll allow, we'll just go on minding our own."

"And who might you be?"

"Mack Lewis."

"What business you down here minding?" Quinn asked Levi, guessing what it was.

"My own."

The punch was short and quick, Quinn getting enough hip into it, his overall size lending it power.

Buckling, Levi was looking at his cap in the street.

Applause and grunts from the men along the wall.

Pointing a finger at Mack, Quinn waited for Levi to pick up the cap, dust it off and rise back up.

"You getting gut-shot down here won't exactly make the papers," Quinn said, stepping close. "Now I asked your business." Half-turning to the men, Quinn watched the grins vanish.

"Guess your social position never rising above a copper," Levi said, "means that crook of a brother's still running the shipyards, huh?"

Quinn's elbow cracked into Levi's middle, doubling him over. His pistol came up, cocked and aimed in Mack's face, Quinn saying, "You'd be kin, I take it?"

Letting the cudgel drop back in his pocket, Mack held his hands wide, saying, "Just down here reliving old times."

Quinn grinned at him, watched Levi pick up his cap a second time, thinking here was the man stole thirty thousand in gold coins, the coins never found.

"The Coast sure can be a hard place on a man." Looking along the line of drunks, Quinn stepped to the sidewalk, liking the fear that had nowhere to hide behind the bloodshot eyes. "Nothing but horse thieves and jayhawks down here. Wouldn't give a fucking eagle for the whole lot. With or without the words 'In God we trust.' Ain't that so, boys?"

A couple of them nodded, some looked away, a few slid down the wall, then Purvis threw up, some landing on Quinn's shoes.

Mack led Levi across the street, helping him along. "Want to tell me what the fuck that was?"

"You mean with Quinn?"

"Yeah, I mean with Quinn. Practically begging him to shoot you."

"Just getting myself geared up."

. . . PEARLY'S GATES

HAIR HUNG in his eyes. The unpracticed tippler leaned on the harlot like a crutch. Lurching under his weight, she steered him past the black slit of an alley running between Pearly's Gates and the Empress Dancehall, two wood-framed Victorian houses of sin, three stories tall, between Stockton and Powell. Both with red porch lights burning.

Feigning amusement at the man's jabber, her horselaugh rose over the two barkers shouting from their stoops, each man in turn promising better entertainment and higher spirits. More red lights burned along the line of dives, tones of merriment carrying from the Melodeon all the way down to the Concert Saloon.

"So, why'd you come back?" Pearly Wilkes asked.

"Why's everybody got to ask that?" Parting the lace of her third-story window, Levi looked out at the ungainly pair weaving in the street. Turning, he tossed his cap on a side table and sat in the armchair. Said no when she suggested he take his boots off, damned things behaving like stubborn corks by end of day, the whiff from his feet likely to make her rethink the offer of the spare room.

Warm eyes and thick lips, big as a man, Pearly placed the cylinder on the Victrola, Nellie Melba's honey voice sounding from the horn. Bringing filled glasses from the desk, she handed Levi one, Old Tom Gin and vermouth with a dash of bitters. Thinking how much he resembled his old man.

He sipped, then picked up the deck and shuffled.

Keeping her elbows tucked tight hid the jiggling flesh under her arms. Pearly knew he was here for the gold coins, likely wanting to buy his place back and reopen it. She said, "Any gal worth her salt'll run you fifteen to twenty a week these days." Sitting opposite, she slid the side table between them, tossing his cap on the rug, dividing some coins in two stacks, adding, "Lord knows it's one shit racket these days, bordellos and cribs springing up like fleas. Not like in Pap's day." She slid one stack toward him.

"Wasn't so easy then, competing with Portsmouth and the Loin," he said. "Thing was, it beat panning, what with bodies floating down the American regular as trout."

She knew the stories from Pap, how he gave up their stake when Levi was just a boy, came to town and opened the Blazes and started fetching gals from the four corners. Women only drunks would spark with, was the way Pap put it.

"In spite of the other joints, this town's always been shy on women, men coming to port all the time," he said. Not like she didn't know it.

Tasting her drink, she asked what came of that old bartender, fellow with the trapdoor.

"Nikko? Took himself a mail-order bride last I heard,"

Levi said, "the woman advertised as untouched and pure as driven snow."

"No shortage of fools." Raising her glass, Pearly toasted him, saying, "You're ducking my question, why you came back."

Dealing two down, one up, he fanned his hand, sliding a coin to the middle, told her what he told Mack.

"Hell, man, I'm serious, every nation on earth's already got one whore in this town." Checking, she looked at him in the lamplight. Five years had taken its toll, lines across his forehead, grey dappling the brown hair. Shoulders more bone than muscle, but still enough there to get a woman's attention.

"Just getting what's mine. Then getting out."

"Had thoughts of it myself. Sick of trying to keep up with what they got going down on Morton. Mexican women for two bits, Chinese, black, French. Take your pick. Get a red-haired Jewess for a buck more. The reason I turned to the boys."

He laid down, ace and king high.

She folded, considered what he said, taking the pins from her hair, shaking the curls down, her own grey hidden from the light coming from over by the desk. "You know what them Healeys are like."

"I do. Fact, I'm counting on it." Looking at the ornate clock, he dealt again, asking after Terrible Terry, remembering the man crusading out front of the Chuck & Luck back in those days, ridding the Barbary of sin. Holding his Good Book, his voice booming scripture, warning of the dens of iniquity and temptation by the serpent, preaching to drunkards and *chilena* whores, anyone who would listen, Levi and Pearly laughing and toasting.

"Called that frontier preaching." Levi showed a pair of sevens.

She threw hers down, finished her drink.

Levi looked at the clock again, thinking any time now.

. . . HEAVY HAND

THE BIG hand shoved the door, Marvin Healey stepping over the barker he'd just laid out with one punch — the man in the middle of saying, "Right this way."

Marvin had the swagger of a man used to having things his way. Dark eyes looking up and down the hall, the crunched envelope in his fist. Stomping to the end of the hall, he yanked back the parlor curtain.

Elmer Epps snapped off the chaise, naked from the waist up, a skinny man of twenty, ribs showing through pocked skin. The book he was reading, *The Virginian*, tumbled to the rug. "Mr. Healey . . . sir?" Pulling off his reading specs, setting them on the table, smoothing his hair, wondering why that fucker Jerrol didn't sound the warning from the front stoop.

"What the hell, Elmer?" Marvin looked dumbfounded at his chief carpenter, then at the book on the floor. "This is a whorehouse, boy, not a damned library." Marvin tugged the curtain closed behind him, the line of photographs displaying the stable of male prostitutes, peeled of their clothing; the last one was of Elmer, his manhood long and limp between his legs.

"I can explain," Elmer said, stepping in front of the photo, stringing together some lies.

"This won't hold water, boy. You're in my employ, for Christ's sake. What would . . ." Taking off his bowler, Marvin set it down, tossed the crushed envelope inside.

"I can explain, sir. It's not something I do on Healey time. You see, my mother's not been —"

The slap knocked him into the wall, the photo dropping from its place.

"Everyone's shitting on me this day, that it?" Marvin said, peeling off his Kohn Brothers jacket, folding it over the chair, popping his cufflinks, tugging up his sleeves.

Elmer went down a wrong road then, saying, "I know it's awkward for you, sir, but I assure you . . . discretion runs in my blood."

Marvin furrowed his brow, Elmer stepping in front and sinking to his knees. Marvin assumed begging was next.

"Strictly confidential sir." Elmer's fingers spidered at the big man's trouser buttons. "My lips are . . . sealed."

Knocked back, Elmer's head struck the wall again, more framed photos falling.

"Marvin Healey's not after your suckering and puckering." Sour at the thought, Marvin had him by the scruff, his rage overtaking him, wrenching Elmer off the floor.

"But sir, you came . . . if not to . . ." Elmer craned his neck, planting a slobbery kiss on the big hand, his second mistake.

Letting go his grip, Marvin grabbed the envelope, ripped it open and pulled out the crumpled photo. "I came for the goddamn Mrs. Healey, you . . ." Waving it in his face. "And if

I find you had your toady hand or worse in her going astray . . ." The thought of this pasty cowpat sticking that part of himself in Marvin's bride was too much.

"No, sir, I never laid —"

The head-butt sent stars, Marvin catching Elmer from falling, holding him at arm's length, venting his frustration.

Elmer was crying and spitting blood, a welt stamped on his forehead. "I would never —"

"Then her goddamned whereabouts best be coming from your sinful lips." Marvin rattled him like a child's toy, hoisting him around, feet in the air. Thumping his fist, smashing Elmer's nose flat. "Think harder, boy. Marvin Healey's a force."

Sputtering blood and something that felt like a tooth, Elmer's pleading became garbled.

Feeling the rush now, Marvin tried reining in his temper. Sure didn't want to call on Quinn to smooth things with the law. Again.

Allowing himself one more, he took Elmer's likeness from the floor, crashing the frame atop the younger man's head, then tossed aside the unholy pervert. Saving the balance of his rage for the missus.

Curled in a whimpering ball, Elmer threw his hands over his head, shards of glass sticking in his hair.

"I asked you the whereabouts of my bride?" Marvin swiped at blood on a cuff, kicking a lace-up Oxford into Elmer's ribcage.

"Upstairs — one of the rooms," Elmer cried, pointing up, blood bubbling from his mouth. Felt the stabbing in his chest, guessing at least one rib was broken, his nose, too. Tongue telling him a second tooth was gone. His looks shot to hell.

Marvin ripped the curtain down, rod, nails and chunks of plaster tearing free. Flinging the mess on Elmer, he stepped on him, picked up his bowler, a new black wool Snellenberg, just in from Philadelphia. Picking up the ruined frame and photo.

"As for your employ, Sweet Nelly . . ." He stepped on Elmer again, tossed the frame down, "consider yourself terminated." Setting the hat on his head, he stepped off the boy, leaving him to his moaning and bleeding. Marvin was warmed up now.

Jerrol the barker stumbled through the door, a hand clapped over his blackened eye. Saw the big man coming down the hall. He tried to move aside. Marvin's punch struck his other eye, knocking Jerrol back out the door, out cold before he landed at the base of the steps.

Grabbing the banister, Marvin clomped up the stairs two at a time, rattling the first door knob he came to.

Locked.

He coiled back, then threw his weight at it, the door ripping from its hinges, crashing in, split down the middle. The doorframe flapping and hanging ragged, splinters forking out from the frame. Marvin stepping through. The smell of fusty perfume and sweaty sex rushed at him.

The shrieking woman bolted up in bed. Jerking the sheet off the naked man like some cheap parlor trick, veiling her jelly breasts. "My time's not up," she bellowed, the light falling across the bed. "Fuck's sakes alive."

Not the missus.

But Marvin recognized the old woman, not the look of someone's sweet nana. "What on God's good earth's . . . Mary Burgess?"

The naked man dove off the bed, scrambling behind the chair, his legs kicking.

"I can explain . . ." Realizing she couldn't, Mary sank her face in her liver-spotted hands.

"Good God, you're shaming your lineage." Marvin turned out the door, sick at the sight, calling back, "Franklin would roll in his grave if he saw this, the poor fellow, married to a tramp."

All that sagging flesh.

He'd see the name of Burgess struck from the membership roster, have her ousted from the San Mateo Club first thing in the morning, the very club he and Franklin founded decades ago, around the time of the first gold rush. Sat in the second row at their wedding.

"You're a horse's ass, Marvin Healey, always have been, busting in on a lady while she's . . . And what you know about my Franklin wouldn't fill your stupid hat." She hurled the oil lamp into the hall, smashing it against the wallpaper, oil spraying up the wall.

Being found in this sinkhole of humankind would ruin her. Healey would wield this, his word enough to grind the name of Burgess under his shoe. No way of knowing the man was here searching for his own wife, the two women sharing a healthy appetite for something neither was getting at home. Their paths never crossing the way they did at the San Mateo Club, where they smiled over lemonade and coffee, offering hellos and nice to see yous, all good and proper.

. . . FLUSH BEATS STRAIGHT

THE CRASHING sounds told him Marvin Healey was here. Levi sipped, watching for the tell. Pearly picked up two, and he knew he had her. There it was, the way she raked her teeth over her lip. He checked the pot, the thudding and yelling coming from one of the rooms downstairs. "Another satisfied customer?"

"The debasing that goes on in this place, nothing surprises me anymore." Pearly guessing Jerrol had things under control downstairs. Studying her cards, she raked her lip. "Like I said, not a business you want to get back in."

More crashing.

"Debasing of the highest order from the sounds of it," Levi said.

"All part of being a house of pleasure," she said, frowning at her cards. "Just play your hand."

"It's to you."

A scream from downstairs, Levi saying it sounded more like terror than pleasure.

Pearly drank her glass down, liking the Old Tom Gin a bit too much these days; this business was getting to her.

"Best I go have a look see," he said, getting up.

"Who you think took care of things the last five years?" She pointed to the axe handle leaning by her door frame. "It's just that Mary Burgess. Woman comes in here and likes to vocalize, kick up her heels. Pay her no mind. Sit." Pearly tossed a coin in the pot, dealing the cards. "She'll pay for her bash, every damn stick she breaks. And you can take that to the bank, goddamn it." Riled up, Pearly tossed her hand down, not her night. "See if I don't give her name to the dailies if she won't make good."

More crashing from below.

Levi couldn't help the grin.

"Pleased with yourself?" she said.

He laid the cards down. Ace on her king high. Five hands straight. "Seems Lady Luck's favoring me tonight."

"Keep it up, you'll be bunking with her . . . out in the alley."

More crashing from below.

. . . TWILIGHT JOHNNY

FLORENCE FULLER Healey assessed herself a trim beauty at forty, gravity not yet the victor. Coming here was affirmation as much as simple pleasure, the silk mask customary in a house like this, making her anonymous while lending a mystery to the whole affair.

She spun Twilight Johnny's chest hair round a painted nail, looking in his eyes from behind the mask in the lamp's glow, the bed slick under them, ignoring the commotion from down the hall. More interested in how this skinny pug-ugly turned her inside out, got her moaning and clawing, peaking her pleasure. Possessing both the ways and the means, something she had found to be rare in a man.

Woody was a spare for when Twilight Johnny needed a rest. Woody was more about the goods, a fine-looking black man, bowed over the edge of the bed, not thinking of putting on his clothes before fishing for his shoes, gripping one with his toes, sliding it to him, shoving his foot into it.

The crashing and thumping down the hall got his attention, something telling him to hide.

It came as an explosion, the hinges ripped from the door. Wood flying in ahead of the lamplight. The coat-rack piled with clothing toppled. All three jolted up, the hall light spilling past Marvin's silhouette. The man breathing hard. Balled fists.

Florence sprang off the bed, her mask flying off, shrieking as he charged in, clouting her with a closed fist, bouncing her off the armoire, no photographer hiding in there now. Tripping over the felled coat-rack, she dropped to the floor.

Woody scrambling against the far wall, paralyzed with fear.

Taking center stage, Marvin planted his feet. No one was getting out of here. Stripping off his jacket, he tossed it at the toppled coat-rack and peeled down his suspenders, huffing air. He had her now.

Tangled in the sheets, Twilight Johnny spilled from the bed to the floor like a sacrifice. Kneeling before the big man, he clasped his hands in prayer. "Now see here, mister, I don't know who you —"

"Then allow me to present myself," Marvin said, his words calm in spite of the whirling storm, lashing out an Oxford, catching Twilight Johnny in the throat, knocking him sputtering into the end of the bed. Snatching him up, Marvin dug his fingers into the pale neck, saying, "I'm Marvin Healey." Looking down at Johnny, not yet limp. "And I see you're already acquainted with the missus."

Air cut off, terror bulged Twilight Johnny's eyes, his mouth flopping open, unable to suck air, unable to speak.

It was a rush Marvin couldn't control now. He slung the suspenders around the scraggy neck, twisting them taut.

Jerking his arm out like a gallows, he strangled Twilight Johnny, the feet sweeping and kicking at the floorboards.

Getting up and charging at Marvin, Florence drummed her fists at him, crying for Woody to do something, Woody frozen in place, back to the wall.

Twilight Johnny pried to get free of the suspenders, tongue hanging out. Marvin jerking him higher, holding him until he hung limp, the sheet slipping away. Florence going at Marvin, crying, punching and digging her claws, raking away his flesh. Biting at him.

Backhanding her, Marvin knocked her into the corner, Florence sliding down the wall, the world spinning.

Inching along the opposite wall like a man on a ledge, Woody snatched at the bed sheet and made for the open doorway. Stomping on the trailing sheet, Marvin stopped him up short. Woody letting go, running naked with one shoe on, yelling down the hall, ping-ponging off the walls, plunging down the stairs, three at a time, going to fetch Jerrol, tripping on the man, losing the shoe, turning and running back up to the top floor, getting Levi.

... A THOUSAND WORDS

ANOTHER SCREAM, then feet pounded on the stairs, preceding Woody bursting through the door, wild-eyed, hysterical and naked, flapping his hands. "He's killing him." Jumping in and tugging at Levi.

Out the door, Levi rushed down the hall, taking the stairs, Pearly grabbing her hickory handle meant for an axe, hurrying after them towards Room 4 and the crashing and screaming. Woody was pointing and shoving Levi in, Pearly winding up.

Inside, Marvin swung Twilight Johnny, rag-doll limp, over to the window. Johnny's head lolled like his neck was rubber, his eyes vacant, tongue and spit trailing from his mouth. Marvin heaved him feet first, smashing out the glass. Nothing more than a glance to the door, Marvin went about ramming Twilight Johnny through the window.

"See you got my photo," Levi said, stepping in, winding his punch. Marvin turned as Levi packed everything into it.

Felt to Levi like he'd struck a sack of beans, doing nothing more than tipping off the man's hat.

Marvin went about letting the body drop to the cobblestones two flights below, inky blood flowing from Twilight Johnny's skull. Marvin turned, remembering who Levi was, sweeping up his hat, setting it on his head.

"You!"

"Wanted you to know . . ." Doubling his fists, Levi came again, windmilling them at the big neck.

Grabbing a fistful of shirtfront, Marvin plowed him back into the wall, Levi sinking to the floor, his vision blurred, feet pedaling to get back up.

Pearly ran and swung the hickory, cracking the big man across the back.

He snatched it from her, his punch catching her square, Pearly flopping into the doorway. Out cold. Tossing the handle into the hall, Marvin grabbed for Woody, Levi shooting out a foot, hooking a leg, causing Marvin to stumble.

Woody hopped over Pearly and was out and down the stairs, enough steam to make it to the opposite coast. Down both flights. Jerrol still lying in the doorway, Elmer crawling along the hallway, his face bloody. Woody reached in Jerrol's pocket, took the man's Iver Johnson pistol, hoping the caliber was up to the job, jumping back up the stairs.

Grabbing a fistful of hair, Marvin yanked Levi up — the man who sent the photo, making a mockery — coiling the suspenders around his neck, dragging him to the smashed window.

"You!"

Pearly was out, and Florence was on all fours, trembling and crawling to the toppled clothes rack.

Ripping at the suspenders, trying to draw air, Levi threw a punch at the brick ribcage. Nothing going to plan.

Marvin struck him, a skull like iron, taking his time now, twisting Levi to face him, this man about to die. Didn't matter he'd be calling Quinn in to clean up the mess. Being choked, Levi lanced his fingers for the big man's eyes, the effect of an irritant bug. Marvin lifted him high with one hand and clouted him with a ham-sized fist. Spidering his arms and legs to keep from being thrown out, Levi seeing two blurry Marvins converge into one. Shoved through the broken glass, he clasped at the frame, hooking the ledge with fingers and feet, shards slicing into his hands.

"You vitiated and syphilized the Healey name for the last time," Marvin yelled at Florence, over his shoulder, "you fornicating bitch." Turning back to Levi, shoving.

Rising behind him, her legs wobbling, blood dribbling between her breasts, her face slick with it, Florence tottered toward Marvin.

Pearly propping herself on elbows at the threshold, pressing up, hearing Woody rushing back up the stairs, seeing it unfold.

"When I finish with you," Marvin said over his shoulder, bundling Levi's arms and legs, thumping his face again, "you won't be mounting the stairs." Marvin thinking he'd kill them all.

Body shaking, Florence raised her arm straight out, finger on the trigger, touching the derringer to Marvin's head.

Feeling the steel, Marvin turned, his teeth in a snarl.

Florence squeezed.

The deafening clap filled the room. Marvin's eyes blew wide, his fingers springing open, blood and brain spouting like an oil derrick, out his ear. His Snellenberg knocked from his head.

Levi tumbled as Florence fired for good measure, the second round not exiting, ricocheting around inside Marvin's skull, the man toppling like a felled oak, blood jetting from the ear.

Plunging two stories, Levi landed on Twilight Johnny. The air knocked out of Levi, Twilight Johnny's lifeless eyes staring at him, blood soaking the ground. Levi tried to crawl off him.

Legs stood like trees before him in the street, but no one came forward. The ground convulsed under him, then consciousness slipped away.

. . . SLIPSTREAMING

In the dream Levi soared, dipping in the air currents above the treetops. Across Folsom Lake and north along the Sacramento Valley, following the bends of the American River. Patches of white showed where the water rushed downstream into blue pools before flowing on. Topping a bluff, he winged over a sawmill, beyond the dogwoods turning color. Men lined the stream, panning for gold.

In the mill's tailrace — the contents of a pan skimmed by a weathered hand — Pap squinted from behind a shaggy beard, picking flakes from the mesh, turning them in the light. His eyes going wide. Bellowing downstream.

The boy looked up from his own pan when Pap started jumping as if possessed. Rushing through the current, the boy fell face first, rising, falling, rising again, splashing his way to Pap.

Father and son arm in arm, guffawing in the stream. Dancing and splashing in the icy water. Fortunes made.

. . . BREAKING A LEG

THE SAILORS rolled their cigarettes outside the Empress Dancehall, base of the steps, too gassed to feel the minor tremor passing underfoot.

The barker at the Empress was Barstow. He ignored the shivering. Striking a match for them, he pulled the door open and wagged them in. "Right this way, gents. Just five cents for real whiskey, two bits a dance. The most beautiful gals in all of Frisco, guarantee you that. And by God, yes, they're good-natured and obliging. Right this way."

Brushing at their clothes, the sailors set foot into the sour-smelling place, five cents ready for the liquid poison being poured. They found space at the bar next to an Indian, rough-looking, with his elbows spread on the polished top. They toasted their pleasure with the first drink. The second was for pluck with the painted ladies.

On the plank floor, couples were stepping, entwined under the dim light and tobacco haze. Sailors, drifters and miners, drunk to a man and swaying with the painted women, the tinny piano and squeezebox setting the tone, two musicians on a makeshift stage of crates, wrecking the tune "Rakes of Mallow."

A woman calling herself Vilvie swayed on stumpy legs, her feet squeezed into beaded shoes, her wild red hair in curls, belly and breasts rocking against a Scotsman. The man wasn't shy about the contact, fingers anchored to her beam, his face pressed into her scented pillows, drawing in her Florida Water. Vilvie let him do it, wagering she'd have him off before she rolled down her silk stockings. Seen his kind a hundred times. Easy start to the night. The Uphams dye in her hair fetching an extra dollar from the man. Redheads known for their fire.

Pulling him in close, Vilvie breathed promises in his ear, flicking her tongue, getting him halfway there, her thigh moving up and down his front, fingers of her free hand brushing the billfold in his back pocket. "You're such a stepper, lover, barely tramping my toes at all." Flicking her tongue again.

The man groaning something.

●

RAWBONED, HAIR looking cut by a blunt hatchet, Red Tom didn't have size, just a look about him that he didn't need it. He downed his whiskey in a gulp. Smacking his satisfaction, he banged the glass on the bar, the two sailors to his left looking at him. Winking to the bartender, Red Tom scoured the room, dropping his coin on the bar. "Wish me luck, boys," he said, straight-arming a path through the dancers, tapping the Scotsman on the shoulder.

Drawing his head from the pillows, the man turned to him.

"I'm cutting in," Red Tom said, his voice a growl, crowding him.

"Sorry, I paid for this dance, friend." The Scotsman's eyes darting around for the bouncer.

"You heathen, go piss off," Vilvie said, shoving Red Tom back. "I ain't stepping with you, told you that more 'n once tonight."

"I'm all man, ain't I?" Red Tom said, raising his voice, eyes burning into the Scotsman like he had pushed him. "All you got to know, my money's good as yours."

"Sure, sure, friend."

"You got no money," Vilvie said, turning and nudging her Scotsman to step up. "Stop bothering me and my man here."

"If the good lady says so," the Scotsman said, "then, I'd take it kindly —"

"Heard what she said." Red Tom drew close, his breath horrible. "Want to know what *you* say, friend?"

"Said I'd take it kindly —"

"Say it again, say kindly one more time, see what it gets you."

The dancing stopped, the two sailors moving like they might step in, the bartender clearing his throat and laying a bat across the wood top, suggesting they finish their drinks, maybe pick out a nice girl, refilling their glasses, this one on the house. The sailors shrugged and toasted the place, watched the dance floor.

"Man just told you to piss off," Vilvie said to Red Tom, pressing her man on. "You don't, my fellow'll boot you out that door."

"Let's have it, then." Red Tom clutched the Scotsman's collar, practically lifted him.

"No, no, I —"

Vilvie egged her man, pressing into him, "Tell him, lover."

"Plenty of the ladies dancing, friend," the Scotsman said. "Sure one would be delighted . . ."

"Show him sand, lover," Vilvie taking his hand, balling his fingers, raising the fist at Red Tom. Vilvie saying, "I just gush when a man's a man."

Grabbing hold, Red Tom twisted and was swinging the Scotsman.

"A man who's a man," Vilvie called, stepping back, giving them room. The other dancers making space, all eyes on the fight.

The Scotsman tried to twist the hand from his collar. Red Tom let him go and took a swing.

Over with a single blow.

Vilvie dropped to her knees, crying and putting the Scotsman's head in her lap, clapping his cheek, the man out cold, catching the smell of his mishap, his bladder having let go. Red Tom dancing a do-si-do around the floor.

House lights flicked off, Vilvie plucking the Scotsman's billfold, relieving him of his cash, tucking it into her cleavage, the empty billfold stuffed back in his jacket.

Lights flicked back on, and Mack Lewis came wading through the dancers, playing the same scene he'd played over and over. Stepping in, he caught hold of Red Tom, whirling him about, saying, "Told you once, told you a hundred times, stay the fuck out of the Empress."

Flashing a knife, Red Tom crouched and circled, everybody backing up more, Mack passing his bowler to a dancer, the bartender tapping the bat on the bar, refilling the sailors' glasses, telling them to stay put and just enjoy the show.

"Gutting you like a fish," Red Tom told Mack, "then I'm having my way."

Ducking, then slugging Tom's jaw, Mack sent him tripping over the prone Scotsman, Vilvie snapping the man's watch from his vest, fingers in every pocket, picking him clean, then tapping his cheek to rouse him.

Spitting a mouthful of blood, Red Tom looked at Mack and came back, swishing his knife, Mack skipping back.

The lights flicked off again, the bartender working the switch.

A collective gasp, the circle widening some more, giving room. Lights back on.

The musicians had stopped mid-tune, the two stepping off the crates and to the bar next to the sailors, breaking for what they called the floor show. Same fight three times a week.

A dark-skinned dancer came off the floor, saying hello to the sailors, telling them she was Honey, stepping between the two, light fingers going into one pocket, then another, the younger of the sailors betting she was real sweet.

All around the dim room, painted and practiced fingers scrabbled into pockets, hooking billfolds, watches and fobs, cash, anything of value. House lights flicking off and on.

Rushing in low, Red Tom arched his blade up and plunged it into a tabletop. Couldn't pry the blade free, Mack coming in and telegraphing a good hook.

Knocked across the table, spilling drinks, Red Tom flipped over and went down in a pile. Sliding the knife to the bar with his foot, Mack plucked the man up, the fight out of him, Red Tom hanging like a sack.

"This sort of behavior ain't tolerated in this fine establishment," Mack called and trucked him by the collar and trousers, across the dance floor and crashing him out the door, pitching him at Barstow's feet, instructing the barker not to let such filth in again.

Then Mack came back in and declared, "Drinks are on the house."

A cheer went up, the merriment recommencing. The bartender obliged, lining them up, pouring watered whiskey, the two-man orchestra taking "Rakes of Mallow" from the top.

. . . THE MEAT AND POTATOES

Waking on the chaise, Levi Hayes felt battered, a pain in every part of him. Sure he was rocking his front tooth with his tongue. The inside of his mouth felt shredded, lip swollen and split. He tried retrieving the dream, but couldn't.

Pearly pulled a chair close, asking how he was.

"How do I look?"

"Serves you right, luring that bull in here." Inspecting his smashed mouth, her own eye black, no amount of blotting powder would hide it. "What in hell were you thinking?"

"I'll make it right."

"Can't get past that pip of a woman doing it," Pearly said, dabbing a kerchief to her tongue, touching it to his lip. "So much for better or worse and till death do us part." Shaking her head.

"Good thing she did, or we wouldn't be having this chat. Ow. Jeez, easy."

"Baby." She kept dabbing. "Let's chat about my place:

smashed walls and window, door busted down, curtains bloody and stains on the floor. Not fit for entertaining. Take days to get it right. Fat chance going after that woman for damages . . ."

"Said I'd take care of it. You see the size of that bull's head?"

"Wish she shot the fool sooner. Saved me a bundle, and Twilight Johnny being my meat and potatoes . . . and Jerrol looking like he's been dragged behind a wagon. Elmer having the man beat right out of him, no good to nobody with a potato for a nose, damn thing bleeding on my Teke rug, shipped it from God knows where."

"Twilight Johnny was a good man," Levi said.

"Yeah, and if you were any younger, I'd make you fill his shoes." Pearly giving a sour look.

"Poor fellow was done when he got thrown out. For sure when I got pitched out on top of him."

"Leaves me with just Woody, and that boy's hardly worth a cotton hat, best of times. Likely hiding in the cellar." She squeezed the cloth over a porcelain basin, dipped it in the pinkish water, dabbed at the cut on his forehead.

"Ow."

"Gonna go baby on me now?"

"How was the state of the grieving widow?"

"Not a tear out of her. Cold as a frost, that one. Put that dinky gun away, got back in her clothes and took the back way out. Picked up the man's hat, all bloody, like it was a trophy." Dipping the cloth, she asked, "What's a reasonable amount of time to go calling on the widow for damages?"

"You're all heart, girl, you know it?"

"It's a house rule, posted right by the door. You break it, you pay for it."

"Leave that with me."

Pressing on the cut, she made him wince. "Why the hell you want to get mixed up with something like her?"

"Lying in the street, she walks by as I came around, bends and asks if I'm able, would I clean up the mess. Come see her after. Make it worth my while."

"Gonna take care of the damages?"

"Told her I'd do it if she'd sign back my deed."

"Aren't you two a pair." Pearly laughed, asking, "And how'd that fare over?"

"Grieving widow asked if I was waiting for him to go ripe."

. . . TREADING THE BOARDS

HOLDING THE door, Barstow ushered the gents into The Empress. The well-to-do didn't often frequent the place, especially sober, these two reminding Mack of the dandy he and Levi spared from the drunkards out front of the Mission. Both in top hats and fine suits, both with wedding bands. Barstow called after them, saying the whiskey was eager and the ladies were flowing, winking at Mack. Mack wondering why a man with a wife at home would come to this place of misery. Get what they weren't getting at home, he supposed, risking returning home with a host of maladies, passing on souvenirs of their visit.

Two of the ladies swooped in, painted and scented, showing cleavage, hooking the gents arm in arm, leading them to the dance floor, asking their names and smiling like old friends. The bartender poured two glasses full.

Mack walked the floor. Vilvie and her Scotsman were swaying cheek to breast, the man forgetting his aches and bruises, not knowing he'd been robbed. Eyes closed, his expression was dreamy. Dropping money and watch into Mack's bowler, Vilvie gave the Scotsman a squeeze, the man groaning, telling her to call him Hamish.

"Evening, folks," Mack said, nodding to another dancer and her embalmed cowboy, the two of them dancing. Holding his hat low, Mack caught a cross on a chain, then strolled to the bar.

"A bonny evening, gents," Mack said to the sailors, the one closest slobbering like an infant on the woman's dress. A billfold dropped into the bowler, Mack smiling and turning. Walking along the bar, he headed for the stairs, moving slow, the other women dropping plunder into his hat, Mack holding it in both hands, careful his pockets didn't jingle.

. . . DOVES AND DAUGHTERS

BYRON BLAKE peered over his turn-pin specs, rejiggering his store-bought teeth, turning his bald head to the window, cupping a hand to his mouth, whiffing his breath, smoothing the goatee. Good enough.

Smiling when the new girl came in, he offered her a place on the settee, taking her in, the girl nervous as a doe. Full-bosomed and of a prime age. Best of all, reddish hair, Byron betting it was red downstairs, something men paid extra for.

Sitting next to her, the fatherly smile meant to ease her, Byron pushed the specs up on his bridge, saying, "Now, did my lovelies explain how this works?"

"Fella at the door just said I should see you." Her eyes darted around the room, the girl having second thoughts.

"Now what did you say your sweet name was?" Byron reached for his ledger on his desk, taking up the pen and dipping it in ink. In a month this one would be just like the rest: cocky, flashing her fanny to any sailor with a dollar to his name, stealing anything she touched. He'd make the extra dollar on account of the hair. Talk around town was Iodoform Kate had retired on a string of redheads, passing them off as Jewesses. Men off the ships sex-starved stupid, paying extra and lining at her door.

"Ethel Biggs," she said, eyes falling to her feet, knees pressed tight.

"That Jewish?"

"Boise, sir."

Frowning, Byron asked her to spell it and made note of it, repeating it, raising his eyes to her. "Biggs might be a name in Kansas, but it's got no distinction for the entertaining business, not in this town."

"Idaho, sir. Where I'm from."

"Yes . . . the name . . . needs to be something more . . . red." He wrote Rose, then scratched it out, thinking something more Jewish. "How's Delilah?" He slid a little closer. "No, not right." Then he had it. "Ruby." It had the right ring. Exotic. Byron writing it down.

"Not sure, sir."

"Best left to me, my dear," he said, patting her arm.

"Mean, me working here."

"Sure, I understand it, but believe me, sweet girl, this place'll grow on you . . . fact, in a week or so, you'll find it inspiring." Catching her scent, something like lye soap. He'd have the other girls get her perfumed up, this one as rigid as pine, her knees locked up tight. "Course I can use inspiring myself from time to time." He swung an arm around her shoulder, drawing her tight. Craning for a kiss, lips puckered, pressing into her.

Being from farm stock allowed her some push-back.

And when he slapped, Ethel slapped back, knocking his turn-pin specs across the room. Springing to her feet, she locked her fingers in fists, Byron trying to catch her hands, elusive as birds. She cracked him across the nose, his eyes watering, Byron diving after her, grabbing a fistful of that red and twisting it to keep her from making for the door.

Shrieking, she fought with her heels, mule-kicking, "I don't —"

"You will."

A yelp of pain.

Byron tried to keep his grip. Twisting her down, he jumped on and pinned her with his knees. "High time you acquired —"

The heel of her hand drove into his crotch.

Air caught in his chest.

An uppercut socked his jaw. He toppled to the floor. Catching her ankle, he kept her from bolting out the door, getting up, dragging her back to the settee, flinging her at it, Byron saying, "So far, not so good." Landing a punch of his own as she tried to rise, unbuckling his belt, pulling it through the loops.

"I'm a dancer, just a dancer." Ethel kicked out at him, Byron catching one ankle, then the other. Then he had her, legs in a V.

"Mr. Blake, please —"

"Now, that mouth best be good for more than back-talk?" Nearly impossible to shove his pants down while hooking her ankles in the crooks of his arms. Pressing her back into the sofa so she couldn't punch.

Then the door flew open. Letting go and diving behind the desk, Byron fumbled the pistol from the drawer. Heard the gunshots earlier from next door, Byron always a careful man. Mack barreled in as if propelled, the doorknob catching in the wall. He'd heard the commotion, guessing what was going on. Face as red as her hair, Ethel got to her feet and stumbled out the door. Crying. Her clothes in disarray.

"Got to be that floor nail," Mack said, letting the girl pass. "Hooked my damned shoe again."

Shaking his head, Byron tossing the pistol back in the drawer, tugging up his trousers, doing up his buttons, looking around for his belt.

"You see my specs?"

Mack looked around, pointed to the floor.

Bending the frames straight, Byron put them on and sat behind the desk, the pain in his crotch suggesting a rupture of sorts. "Knock, goddamn it, Mack. Know I conduct my business up here. And you've got hung on that same fucking nail how many times now?"

"Sorry about it, boss. Keep forgetting."

"How about you take a fucking hammer to it. That be too hard?"

"Sure thing."

"I can't give these gals a fair and proper assessment with you falling through the door, getting caught on the same fucking nail." Byron thinking he'd better send Vilvie for some ice. "Just asking for some consideration for Christ's sake. These girls are your bread and butter, too."

"Said I'll keep in mind to pound it down." Mack emptied his bowler of what the girls had poached, spilling it on the desk. Digging in a pocket, he added some bills and stacked some coins. "Brought up the night's take is all. You're always ragging on me to bring it straight away."

Plucking up a billfold, Byron turned it out. "How much my beauties abstract tonight?" Dumping out two more, counting the plunder, losing his smile, he recounted, saying, "Twelve fucking dollars and a cheap watch?" Pocketing the bills, he tossed the billfolds in the trash under the desk, the bin overflowing with them. Worst night in a week. He shook his head. "Twelve maggoty dollars? What am I gonna do with . . ." He put the watch to his ear.

Mack had already gone out the door.

"I'm being hoodwinked by whores," Byron said it loud. "Bitches failing to render true account." Shaking the watch, putting it to his ear again. "Hardly worth keeping the doors open." Tossing it in the bin. "Soon I'll be resorting to male whoring, like that sow next door." Getting up, he hobbled for the door, scooping the belt from the floor, sending it through the loops, thinking he ought to go see Doc Burrows. Pulling the knob from the wall, he stuck his head out the door, calling down the stairs, "And pound down that fucking nail once and for all."

Yelling for ice, he slammed the door, groaning from the hurt that followed, getting back behind the desk, sinking in his chair, reaching for the bottle in his lower drawer.

. . . THE DEEP SIX

GLASS CRUNCHED underfoot, Levi looking up at Pearly's boarded window. A two-flight drop to the cobblestones. Twilight Johnny had broken his fall, the dead man allowing Levi to limp away. The poor fellow naked and dead in the street, his blood staining the stones. Jerrol and Elmer had been quick getting the body off the street and out of sight. Tossing a bucket of water on the blood, avoiding undue attention.

Walking to the alley now, Levi caught sight of Woody walking up Pearly's front steps, swaying with a bottle in hand, Jerrol helping him inside. The alley between Pearly's and the Empress was narrow and in pitch. Levi put aside his aches. One Healey sent to his maker, any pain was worth that.

Air thick with piss and vomit. His eyes adjusted to the pitch. The sound of someone being kicked, a voice yelping out. He flattened against the wall, hard breathing and shuffling coming his way. A vagrant bumped past him, smelling horrible, grumbling and hurrying out into the street.

A light came on in an upstairs window of the Empress, casting down the clapboard walls, the silhouettes of Mack and Red Tom at the end of the alley. Leaning against opposite walls, rolling smokes.

"Gotta hold some back," Red Tom was saying to Mack, "like we talked about." Demonstrating the punch with a swivel of his hips, he stopped short of Mack's chin. "Like that."

Chewing Juicy Fruit, Mack said, "Point of it is, Tom, it's gotta look convincing. Fellows may be drunk, but they ain't all stupid." Looking up, saying hey to Levi.

Levi taking a spot against the wall.

"Still, a feller's only got so many teeth," Red Tom said, nodding to Levi, then saying to Mack, "Just ease up a bit, is all I'm asking."

Mack said he'd treat him like the delicate flower he was, reaching in a pocket, taking a fistful of bills, counting out half of what he'd held back from Byron, handing the share to Red Tom. "Ought to be enough to cheer you and leave plenty for your dental concerns."

"Well now," Red Tom said, "guess we can let things slide," counting out nine dollars, tucking it away, a far cry from the twenty cents Byron paid him for an hour of sweeping and mopping puke off the dance floor, acting like the crazy Indian. "You're a fine fellow, Mack, got the knuckles of old Jack Johnson, but for this kind of dough, suppose you can club me all you want."

Mack held out the makings, Levi taking the pouch and papers, rolling a smoke, Red Tom striking a match, the three of them puffing, smell of tobacco masking the piss and vomit.

"Run into Healey again?" Mack asked, seeing Levi's swollen eye in the match light.

"Big brother Marvin this time."

64

"Goddamn, you got to get them all beating on you to get you in the spirit?" Mack guessing Marvin Healey got the envelope, figured out who dropped it off. Things not working out like Levi wanted.

"Surprised you boys didn't hear the shots."

"Shots? Jeez, hell's sure got a way of dogging you," Mack said.

"Tell you about it while you lend a hand," Levi said, drawing on the smoke. "Got a delivery to make."

"Delivering what?"

"Marvin Healey."

It took a second. Mack said, "You shot him?"

"His missus did that. One of them derringers." Levi showing the size of the gun with his hand. "Marvin comes storming in all on fire —"

"On account of your photo."

"Set him off some," Levi said, Red Tom asking, "What photo?"

Levi saying, "Man busts in, catches her with Twilight Johnny and Woody, the three of them on the bed."

"Jesus."

"Yuh, anyway, the man takes to choking the Jesus out of Johnny, throwing him out the window by the time I got down the stairs. Knocked Pearly out cold. Was beating on me, chucking me out after Johnny when the missus sticks her dainty barrel in his ear."

"And shot him?"

"Both barrels."

"That's some woman," Red Tom said, thinking he'd seen her around.

"You get the deed?"

"Right after we dump the stiff."

65

"Well, if the fellow's dead," Red Tom said, "he'll keep fine till morning. I'm in no way fit for digging holes tonight. Sore as hell."

"A fiver says it's tonight." Levi dug in a pocket for some bills, saying, "Just got to ready a skiff and row the bodies out, drop them in the Bay."

"Saying you got more than one?" Red Tom asked.

"Healey and Twilight Johnny." Levi held out a bill.

"Where you suppose I'm gonna find a cart this time of night?"

Levi waited.

"Call it a fiver each, and never mind one's the size of two men." Red Tom dragged on the smoke, letting Levi decide, the red glow looking like a firefly with a tail.

Levi peeled off another bill, wagging them, saying, "Tonight."

"Tonight." Snatching the bills, Red Tom summed it to the night's take. Not bad considering the average joe made two hundred a year. Grinding his smoke with a heel, he said, "One burial at sea coming up." Moving from the alley, rotating his shoulder.

"Who we gonna blackmail now?" Mack said.

"Told you, the wife's signing it over."

"Suppose we can trust her?"

"We got the leverage. Pearly and me witnessed the killing. Half-dozen others saw him storm in, most of them beaten to hell. Works out none too bad. Healey blood's been spilled, without us doing any of the spilling. And we get back the deed."

"How about Quinn?"

"Time comes, I'll take care of him."

66

. . . FEEDING THE LEOPARDS

Fog ROLLED across the Bay, shrouding the lights from the Oakland shore. Boards on the pier were slick underfoot. A flag flapped from an outhaul, waves lapping at the pilings dotted with mussels and barnacles. The waterfront off East Street lay deserted, not a dockhand around at this hour. No lights along the row of buildings, giving the place the eeriness of a cemetery, a forest of masts sticking beyond the stack of an iron ship.

Levi lifted Twilight Johnny, roped and wrapped in sack cloth, from the cart and draped him over his shoulder. He trudged under the weight, careful of his footing. Mack and Red Tom struggled to get Marvin from the bottom of the cart, Mack taking the shoulders, Red Tom at the feet, the two of them arguing about the best way to navigate something this size. Marvin's ass dragged on the ground. Red Tom going on about not being paid nearly enough. "Fine for Johnny, but this Healey fellow's size of a fire engine."

Climbing down a rope ladder, Levi planted a foot in the

skiff, easing Twilight Johnny into the bottom. Lowering the body to the dock, Mack lifted a shoulder, Red Tom shoved Marvin with his foot, off the pier, the big body landing on top of Johnny's, nearly capsizing the skiff.

"Take it fucking easy," Levi said, grabbing the dock piling. Red Tom shrugged.

A tremor rattled the pier, all three looking at each other, then getting back to work.

Hoisting a slab off the pier, Mack passed it down to Levi, the skiff dipping, swaying side to side. Shoving the slab under Twilight Johnny's sheet, Levi trussed him with a rope. A second slab was laid on Marvin, Levi securing the knots, thinking somebody should say a few words, nobody knowing any. Then he climbed up on the pier.

"Poor bastards," Red Tom said, going down the ladder, settling between the bodies. "I go before you boys, I don't want no watery grave."

Looping the end of the bowline, Mack tossed it in, Red Tom pushing an oar off the piling, rowing into the fog.

"We'll stick your stiff ass in the ground, don't you worry about it," Mack said, looking around, making sure they weren't seen.

"Don't want to be eaten by maggots neither," Red Tom said. "Pomo need to be set afire. Frees the spirit so we meet up with our ancestors and become immoral."

"Got no worries about that," Mack called. "Most immoral bastard I ever met."

Levi and Mack grinning.

They lost sight of him in the fog, heard him hauling on the oars, the swish and squeak, still going on about two fivers not being enough pay, Levi asking what the hell a Pomo was.

"The kind of Indian he is."

. . . ON THE HOOK

OPENING HIS shirt, Levi checked the bruises, the one across his chest big and purple. "Getting too long in the tooth to get chucked out of windows. Every inch of me's suffering one pain or another."

"Brought it on yourself," Pearly said, Levi on her chaise again, Pearly back to playing doctor.

The knock on the door startled them both. Getting up, Pearly went for the hickory handle, then opened the door a crack.

Worried look on his face, Woody stepped in, saying, "The other Healey's downstairs."

"The widow?"

"The brother."

Tugging Woody into the room, Pearly shut the door. "Why the fuck didn't you say I wasn't here."

"Just told me to go fetch you," looking at Levi, "wasn't using your Christian name, neither."

"He can't know anything," Pearly said. "Man just wants his money."

"Then why's he asking for me?" said Levi. "And what money?"

Taking cash and a derringer from a drawer, Pearly went for the door, saying, "Nothing to trouble yourself about."

"Looking-the-other-way money?"

"I'll take care of it."

Levi snatched the money from her, saying, "Least I can do."

"Think you done enough."

"Gonna get suspicious, he sees that eye." Levi pointed. "You being a lady."

"Not so pretty yourself."

"He'd expect it of me," Levi said, taking the derringer. "And what's this for?" A double-barreled .41-caliber Colt. Could fit in a child's hand, packing double the wallop of Florence's .22, drop an ox like Quinn at close quarters.

"Case the money ain't enough," Pearly said. "I'm a little shy this week."

Tucking it into his waistband, Levi flapped his shirt over it, following Woody into the hall, thinking he should shoot Quinn and get it done, pay Red Tom another five to row him out, dump him with his brother, fatten up the leopard sharks.

●

PASTING ON the man-without-a-care deportment, Levi stepped past the parlor curtain, pulling it closed behind him, leaving Woody in the hall with Jerrol, and said, "Officer Quinn, nice of you to call."

Wiping a kerchief over his brow, Quinn looked at the photos lining the wall, three of them with cracked glass, saying, "Turns my stomach to think of men whoring themselves. Just not natural."

"Ought to give it a try."

"You recommending it?"

"Me, I'm just visiting."

"Got a mind to shut this shit-stable down. Be done with the lot of you."

"Then you'd have to go sticking your hand in somebody else's pocket." Levi tossed the bills on the table.

"Think that's a problem? The Barbary's got more whorehouses than churches," Quinn said, making no move for the money, playing the copper, noting the broken picture frames, bits of glass and bloodstain on the rug. "See your upstairs window's busted and boarded."

"Pigeon flew into it."

"Then flew in your face?" He pointed at Levi.

"Fool came in, needed sorting out."

"Not a quiet night, then?"

"We get a quiet night, you'll know when your cut dries."

"That's two; third time gets you hit again," Quinn said. "And so we're clear, I get paid for looking the other way. Don't get paid for turning a blind eye."

"How much a blind eye go for these days?" Levi grinned, ready.

Eyes on him, Quinn gathered the bills and tucked them away, saying, "She's short."

"May be, but she's still something."

"I come back tomorrow, tell her to bring it down herself. And she can make up for me having to come twice."

Both staring, both ready.

. . . UNDERTAKING

A MAN of servitude, Hamish the Scotsman fixed his eyes on the plank floor, feeling bad for getting robbed down at the Empress, guessing Mack Lewis had a hand in it — just couldn't help going down there, drinking and dancing with those girls. He ushered Levi and Mack into Marvin Healey's office, a private suite at the far end of the block-long building. The sounds of the shipyard ringing from outside.

Recognizing the Spanish chandelier hanging in front of a paned window as his own, taken from the House of Blazes, Levi stepped in, crossed a grizzly-head rug, saying Florence Healey had a nice view of the Bay.

From behind Marvin's desk, in reverie with a ledger, Florence glanced up, giving him a weary look, her rouge doing a fair job hiding the contusion and bruise. The younger one by the door looked related.

Her coiffed poodle, Precious, sat up in its wicker basket next to the desk, a red kerchief around her throat.

Whimpering. The poodle and kerchief were the only signs that a woman had ever set foot in this room, the walls sporting a buck of fourteen points, a bull elk and a trophy billfish. A gun case stood near the window, boasting a Marlin lever-action, a Remington flintlock, a pair of Springfield trapdoors, Hawken muzzleloader and a Hatfield sporting rifle.

"What can I do for you, gentlemen?" Looking up with a banker's indifference, Florence dipped her pen in an ink bottle and scratched some figures.

Levi and Mack traded looks.

"It's about the deed, ma'am," Levi said, taking off his cap.

"A deed?" Jotting an entry, considering what she'd written, she blew before flipping it closed, sighing and looking up. "Shall I just guess the rest?"

"Come now, Mrs. Healey, we had an arrangement," Levi said, stepping to the desk, not liking the way this was going.

Taking out a sheet of rose-colored crepe paper, putting it to her lips, she said, "If you think I have time for games, mister . . ."

"Know damned well who I am."

"Read about someone like you some years back, something about stealing gold from the Mint, am I right? Now, here you are without an appointment while my husband's at sea."

"Making it sound like he's on it, instead of under it." Pulling out the chair opposite, Levi looked at Marvin's Snellenberg on the seat, bloody inside. He picked it up, saying, "Goes nice with the rest of the trophies." Tossing it down, he eased into the chair, saying, "I understand you're bereft with grief, ma'am, but there's still the matter of compensation."

Her mood lightened. Sitting back herself, she allowed him his moment.

"That is, if you want us keeping hush." Raising his boot, setting it across the corner of the desk.

Mack stayed by the door, hand on the knob; none of this was going according to plan.

"See, ma'am, there were some unexpected expenses in the removal of your dearly beloved."

That brought a smile. Her teeth white, straight and perfect.

"Let's call it fifteen even." Levi took an interest in a smudge on the heel of his boot, licking, then rubbing a thumb over it. "See, your mister's bulk required extra hands."

The smile couldn't hide her wintry bearing. "Let me get this right, sir, you wish to extract a fee for . . . oh, this is a stitch."

Her laugh caused Precious to yelp, the dog spinning in its basket, sensing its mistress's slow burn.

"Might want to think how this'll sound to your brother-in-law, Quinn. I'm guessing, he gets wind how you splashed his brother's brains against a whorehouse wall — well, I dare say it'll fetch you more than a stitch across your pretty little nose."

Mack said that's right and turned the doorknob, wishing this were over.

"You think it's pretty?" Touching her nose, she stood and went past the gun case, turning with mock horror, putting on a show. "Oh, my good Lord." The back of her hand to her forehead, looking like she might pass out.

Levi and Mack exchanged looks, Precious hastening the circles at Florence's feet, whimpering a storm.

"You need salts, ma'am?" Mack asked.

"Pray tell you brutes haven't brought harm upon my poor Marvin?" Voice choked, the look of a woman who'd seen a

74

terror, she pointed a finger at Levi, then at Mack, clapping a hand to her trembling lip.

The dog yapped and spun.

"No kind of harm could be brung on him once you . . ." Levi put a finger gun to his ear, pulling a pretend trigger. Then swinging his boot down, he got up, Mack with the look of a panicked steer, the dog spinning faster, its whimpering turning to a low howl.

Tears streamed down the woman's cheeks, her hand stretching out like a sponger's.

"You a thespian, ma'am?" Mack said, hand pushing open the door.

Pulling a hanky from a silver case on the desk, she shut the waterworks, dabbed at her cheeks. "I assure you gents, my lament will be doubly convincing after I've rehearsed the thing a time or two. And I'll have Quinn and the fine jury sequestered at your trial lapping it up." She flipped the hanky at the hat on the floor, went and sat behind the desk, saying, "Likely lynch you right on the courthouse steps."

"Come now, Mrs. Healey," Levi said, "nobody in their right mind —"

"Just try me, Mr. Hayes. I'll see you two swinging for it. Isn't that how your ilk usually ends up, swinging from a rope?"

"You forgetting about eyewitnesses?"

"A screaming nigger halfwit and his drunken madame. Oh, and you, a convict sentenced for robbing the U.S. Mint, against me, a long-standing pillar and close friend of our beloved E.E. Schmitz. She snapped her fingers. "Where's that leave you, Mr. Hayes? And you . . ." Looking at Mack.

"I'm getting that deed," Levi said.

"Not in this lifetime." She called out, "Hamish, get in here!"

Precious circled, her cries hysterical. The door opened, the Scotsman easing past Mack, standing at attention.

"Unless you're more man than meets the eye, go fetch Van Doy," she said. "I want these hooligans rousted from the premises."

"Yes, Mrs. Healey." Hamish glanced at the men as way of warning, spun on his heels and was underway.

"A gesture of fair play, gents," she said. "My man Van Doy is a neckless creature with a taste for inflicting hurt. I suggest you vamoose, or mosey, or sashay as fast as you can." Florence lifted her pen, getting back to the ledger. "And you can forget about that deed. Now and forever. Don't know what the dickens you'd want with that wreck anyway — another house of ill-repute, I suppose."

"You think it's over?"

"Trouble is, you don't know when you're bested, Mr. Hayes."

Flicking a foot at the poodle darting in and nipping at his pant cuffs, Levi put his cap back on, saying, "Oh, uh, a suggestion for you, ma'am. Next time the need to be rode hard and put away wet hits you, you best make use of this neckless Van Doy fellow."

She made a wild throw, the ink bottle bursting against the paneling, flecking Precious, the wall and the rug. Levi smiled, turning and going down the stairs, feeling the meeting hadn't been a total thrashing.

... THE GIBSON GIRL

HER HAIR tucked under the hat, Gibson-girl style, Florence was perfumed and dressed in finery, the tea gown from Paris, passementerie and long white gloves, pearls doubled around her neck. A beauty at forty. Tilting the parasol on her shoulder, Florence Healey led Precious into the perfect afternoon. The loss of Marvin making her stroll across the manicured grounds more agreeable than usual, an afternoon ritual past the beds of perennials, predominantly purple with clusters of yellow lilies this time of year.

Through the iron gates, she turned and took in the vast estate. Daniel H. Burrington, Marvin's double-chinned architect, proclaimed the Healey property had no rival on Nob Hill, or anywhere else on God's green earth. The stained glass, the carriage house, the portico, the finely detailed corbels and columns. All belonging to her now, soon to be seen as the grieving widow. She considered sending for black attire, something from the studios along Rue Halévy or Place Vendôme.

Quinn would get in the way. Next in line to run the ship-yard. She paused and considered it. Perhaps Van Doy would take care of him, come from behind one night. An officer of the law led a dangerous life.

Florence meant to have it all: the estate, the shipyard, the Ocean Shore, the McCloud River Railroad, Shevlin Lumber, the Ash Creek Mill. She had perused the ledgers, would set a meeting with the lawyers, the accountants and managers. Now all in her employ.

She touched a gloved hand to her nose, a fractured carti-lage the doctor called it, well worth the price of her freedom. The whip-hand, Marvin liked to call himself. Most satis-fying moment he gave her was the stupefied look, the light going from his eyes, dropping like a steer before the abat-toir's hammer.

Talk of his disappearance would fade, her rancor would fade, too, and soon she wouldn't think of him at all.

A wall bordered her grounds. Outside it a navy man leaned his pressed blues against the stones. Unusual in this neighborhood, Florence recalling tales of larceny circulating at the club, sailors on the drunk breaking into estates of the well-to-do, holding blue-bloods at gunpoint, demanding a ransom. Could be this one already heard rumors of her recent widowhood, the nearby Barbary being no place for secrets?

Giving the parasol a twirl, she strolled along the wall, the reloaded derringer in her tiny bag. The sailor glancing her way, rolling a cigarette. Lighting up, he smiled and nodded a hello, waving out the match. Tall, dark and strapping, with an angular jaw.

She stopped, allowing Precious to sniff his trouser leg. "You lose your way, sailor?"

"G'day, miss." Deeply tanned, skin rough, creases at the

corners of his eyes when he smiled. The broad shoulders and hands that had known labor. She guessed him to be shy of forty, but couldn't place the accent.

Tilting her head in a way she thought men found playful, Florence said, "You sound a long way from home."

"That's a fact, ma'am. Halfway round the globe, in fact. Perth, Australia, to put a pin on a map." Dragging on his smoke. Eyes meeting hers. Lingering.

"Far from your loved ones."

"True enough." Reaching down, he let Precious sniff his hand, stroking her head, his eyes running along the tea gown, not being shy about it. Rising up. "Sure a fine-looking pooch you got, ma'am."

"That's kind of you to say, sir." His boldness amused her. The two of them standing close.

"Got one back home myself."

"A pooch?"

"More of an old collie dog, named her Maggie."

Back home with the missus and a bunch of kids, no doubt.

"Your pooch got a name, ma'am?"

"Call her Precious."

He smiled, saying he was Liam Preston. "At your service." Bending again, patting the dog's head, looking up at her. "Seems Precious likes to be stroked."

"Seems you have a way . . . stroking."

Liam straightened and turned, dragging on the smoke. Hardly a foot between them now.

She took it from his mouth, taking a puff, giving a slow exhale in his face, the man not bothered about it.

He knew Levi and Mack would be in the house now. Wooing this woman was turning out to be child's play; still, the hunger in her eyes was unnerving Liam. Hired to delay her on her daily stroll. Conversation or cock, whatever kept her busy. Five dollars either way, the money he'd pick up on his way past Pearly's, on his way back to his ship. Be back onboard by the time this woman realized she'd been robbed. Liam would depart from this godforsaken place, his ship sailing for Juneau. Maybe find work up there in some lode mine. Too many crazy people in this town.

Slipping the cigarette back between his lips, she was about to speak, then her eyes went wide, and she took a step back. Composing herself.

The look on her face sent hackles up the back of his neck, Liam sensing someone behind him. Turning.

Officer Quinn stepped between them, brass buttons polished and hat straight on his head. Looking from one to the other. A bouquet held behind his back.

"Why, Quinn, what an unexpected surprise. What brings —"

Presenting the flowers with a flourish, he said, "Evening, Florence. This sailor lose his sense of direction?"

Accepting them, she put her nose to the blooms, gaining composure. "No, this seaman's been just delightful. Taking a liking to Precious, and her to him."

"Huh."

"Just strolling through Nob Hill, taking in the sights, exchanging pleasantries," Liam said.

"From Perth, Australia, I believe you said, that right, mister . . ." Florence pretending to fish for his name.

"Preston. Liam Preston." Offering his hand to the copper.

Quinn looked him over, ignoring the hand, asking, "Which ship you fall from?"

"Came on the *Pride of Perth*."

"A freighter?"

"Yes, sir, and a fine one at that. Going north on the Klondike with Skookum Jim, ship's being loaded as we speak."

"That a fact?"

"Yes, sir. Took advantage of the time for a stroll through your fair city, stretch these legs, the good lady here instructing me on the quickest route back. Easy enough to lose track in this maze of streets, taking in all these fine houses."

"Navy man serving on a freighter?" Quinn looking at the uniform.

"Guarding currency for the mining going on up in Fairbanks. Fact, judging by the sun, I best make tracks. Jim'll be wondering what became of me. Setting sail first light, and still got plenty to do."

"Bet you do."

Tipping his cap, Liam hoped Levi and Mack were close to done, not getting his chance with the woman, but relieved about it just the same, saying, "Nice talking to you, ma'am," then to Quinn, "G'day, Officer. Cheerio, Precious." A quick pat to the dog's head, then he was heading along the stone wall, going down the hill.

"Very thoughtful and kind of you to call, Quinn." Nose back in the blooms, Florence watched Liam disappear past the hedge.

Pity.

"Seems I'm the center of attention this day," she said. "But, I suppose you've come to see Marvin."

"As a matter of fact, I have," Quinn said, having gotten word she'd spent yesterday alone at the office, and guessing his brother was out of town. Looking at her nose, he guessed his asshole brother had taken a hand to her, again. The woman giving him another set-to. Catching her alone, Quinn was hoping for his chance. Have his own set-to.

"Poor boy was so fired up, he neglected to say when he'd return," Florence said, glancing back to her gate.

"Yeah, know how he is."

"Fact, I suspect they just laid the keel for the *Star of Bengal*. Marvin's unable to resist a maiden voyage, likely en route for San Diego. In the buzz of it, he likely forgot to get word to me. That man can be so like an excited child, the dear boy." She smiled.

"In that case, allow me to escort you back to your door." Quinn offered his arm, turning her through her gate, saying how nice her gardens were looking.

"Why, thank you," she said, then, "Would you favor a tea, Quinn?" Touching her hair, adding she was afraid she'd sent all the servants home, the two of them left on their own to brew it.

"Think we can manage a pot of tea, don't you?" Quinn smiling.

"I'm just certain of it." Florence squeezing his arm, curious to see where this was going.

•

THE ROW of yew concealed him, Mack Lewis shoving at the stubborn window, banging it with his palm, sticking his head inside. It felt wrong — like breaking into hell. That look on Florence Healey's face at her office had him unnerved. The way she'd stood in front of Marvin's gun case, putting on the theatrics with the trophy heads looking on. The bloody Snellenberg on the floor.

Hoisting himself to the sill, he looked back at Levi. Could be his uncle had lost his mind. Five years in San

Quentin could do that to a man. Pulling himself through, Mack tumbled to the floor. The marble cold and hard.

Not a sound but the clack of the tall-case clock at the far end of the hall, the soaring ceiling reminding him of a childhood fairy tale — the place where Jack's giant lived. A rich man's place, likely had an indoor bathtub like Levi had talked about, these people pissing inside their own four walls.

Slinking through, he walked past statuary on pedestals from the Ming and Tang dynasties, Chinese bronze, African jade on pedestals, their value lost on Mack. He went and unlatched the servant's entrance.

Closing the door behind him, Levi glanced about like an appraiser, telling Mack to look sharp. Mack following down the same hallway of Dutch Masters and Flemish baroque, a string of family portraits looking on, bearing witness. Ornate woodwork, fine marble, crystal and brass fixtures and stained glass.

Neither had ever seen anything like it, treasures worth a king's ransom, all ripe for the pluck. Levi set to take back what he was owed. And then some.

Shoving a sack into Mack's hand, he got to work, starting in the butler's pantry, emptying a cabinet of anything looking of gold or silver: a candelabra, a server, a couple of chargers, telling Mack, "Just shit that won't break. Stuff with a shine."

Setting to work on the cabinet's twin on the other side of the doors, Mack dropped a Buddha in his sack, the drawers giving up handfuls of silver cutlery with ivory handles. Levi going, "*Shhh*" on account of the clanking.

Took about a minute, Levi hefting and tallying about thirty pounds of loot, thinking he should have brought extra sacks.

. . . QUIBBLE THE TOSS

SHE SLIPPED on the green silk, mail-ordered from New York, the corset tight as skin, advertised to knock off ten pounds, likely took off as many years, too, giving her what the ladies called a wasp's waist. Fussing in front of the dressing mirror with Nellie Melba playing on the Victrola, Pearly was set to do some stepping out on the town. She planned to put a bug in Levi's ear, get him to escort her to the Palace Grill. A fine steak supper under candlelight, drink some champagne from a flute, then take in some opera. Heard Caruso was in town, performing *Carmen*, in the role of Don José. Be a perfect evening. Her barker Jerrol had his means. Might be able to get tickets on short notice, get Levi into some befitting wear. A carriage ride to the top of Telegraph Hill would be a nice finish to the evening, see the lights of the city. Talk about old times.

With Woody in tow now, Pearly stepped out on her porch. Woody was playing the unwanted shadow, talking her ear off, holding recent occurrences responsible for his inability to get back to work. She was sick of hearing his excuses, flaccid being no good to anyone. One boy dead, two laid up, and one plain useless. She'd end up in the poorhouse at this rate. She truly needed a night on the town to clear her mind.

•

SICK OF the stale tobacco and perfume filling the place, Byron Blake stepped from the Empress next door, his barker Barstow not in his usual spot. A golden voice that could bellow to the next block, the man had become lost to the hop of late, likely lying in some Chinese crib, his mind turned to porridge. Byron decided to get rid of him. Run an ad for a new man.

Twenty feet away, Pearly stood on her own stoop in some green get-up, Byron thinking she looked ridiculous. Nothing feminine about the big-boned creature. Not a kind word between them in a dozen years, a bitterness time hadn't eased. The black one called Woody was whining about some travesty that had befallen him, Byron quick to guess its nature.

"Perils of the gender, my boy," he called over to Woody. "Happens to the best of us, or so I'm told." Grinning, saying, "Not an affliction I've ever contended personally, mind you."

Knuckles at her wasp's waist, she said, "Then you'll have no problem going and fucking yourself."

Would like to shoot that woman, see her buried in that green get-up. Byron gave a tight smile back, going through his door. He looked across the smoke-filled dance floor of his own establishment, his eyes falling on Vilvie at the bar, her fat foot up on the rail, talking to the bartender, waiting for some johnny to just wander in. He needed to yell at her, just couldn't think of a reason yet.

Stomping across the dance floor, he told her he wanted to see her — now — taking the stairs, catching his shoe on the floor nail on the landing, pitched into his office.

Following, Vilvie kept a straight face, lifting her shirts over the threshold, guessing what she was in for, closing the door behind her.

. . . JOHNNY LAW

AN OIL painting of a man on horseback wouldn't fit in the sack. Mack tried poking a thumb through the canvas eye of great-grandfather Healey, hanging it crookedly back on its nail. Sweeping through the dining room to the foyer, a room on either side of the circular staircase, both dark with the drapes drawn. Starting up the stairs, Levi guessed Healey might have some ill-gotten cash stashed up in the bedroom someplace.

Midway up, they froze.

The sound of laughter coming from just outside the door, growing louder. A woman's voice, then a man's. Hustling back down on tiptoes, they made for the servants' entrance.

The door knob rattled, the two of them ducking into the butler's pantry, tucking behind the double doors, Levi behind one, Mack behind the other, scarcely daring to breathe, pulling the sacks tight to their bodies, both wondering what the fuck happened to Liam. The man was supposed to have a way with the ladies.

•

SHUTTING THE door, Florence and Quinn stood in the marble foyer. Giggling at his wit, she excused herself to put the flowers in water, see about some tea, leaving him holding Precious. Walking down the hall, she passed the butler's pantry, heels clanking on the cold floor. Tossing the cheap flowers in the kitchen bin.

Watching her through the crack between the door and frame, Levi felt sweat bead on his brow, Pearly's derringer in his pocket — doubting he could shoot a woman, even this one. He tried turning his head the other way, couldn't see the man by the front door, thinking it was Liam, coming in too soon, but then heard him talking baby-talk. Levi recognizing the voice of Officer Quinn.

Baby-talking to Precious, Quinn held her up, assuming the growl was meant for him, not aimed at the thieves behind the pantry doors not fifty feet away. Thinking the dog was picking up his carnal intentions for her mistress, the man craving his own brother's wife. The dog being loyal to its master. Stroking her, Quinn said it was alright, and what a good dog she was, thinking there wasn't much to her neck under the curled fur.

Taking Florence in as she came back down the hall, her hips rocking, the thin waist, the breasts. Marvin out of town. With any luck, the son of a bitch would slip off the deck and be reported lost at sea.

"Afraid I can't locate the tea," she said. "How about we skip right to something stronger?"

"Now you're talking."

Taking Precious from him, she said she kept the good

stuff up here, taking the stairs. "Hope I'm not luring you into any kind of trouble with your superiors," she said, adding, "Your being on duty and all."

"Assure you, that's not the case," he said, following her up, taking two stairs at a time, his eyes glued to the back of her dress.

●

LEVI FELT the floor shake underfoot. Eyeing Mack through the door's crack. The fixture over the dining table swayed on its linked chain. What they hadn't plundered rattled in the twin cabinets.

Upstairs a door closed, then quiet.

"What the fuck was that?" Mack breathed.

"*Shh.*"

Neither dared to move.

Levi waiting, finally guessing Quinn and Florence were getting biblical, giving sufficient time for them to engage. He poked his head out, keeping his voice low, "Let's get gone." Stepping into the hall, Mack right behind him.

Tiptoeing down the hall, Levi planned to come back another time, grab some more of this stuff. It was the growling that stopped him, looking back at Precious at the top of the staircase, the dog baring its teeth, Levi making *shhh* sounds, saying in that low voice, "Nice doggie," back-pedaling down the hall, past the art treasures.

From upstairs, Florence yelled for Precious to shut the fuck up, Precious swooping down the stairs, charging and yelping, snatching hold of Mack's pant leg, rat-shaking her head, the red kerchief flapping.

Kicking at her, Mack swatted with the sack, missing, Precious hysterical, going at the intruder, jumping in, darting out, tearing at the pant leg, snapping her teeth at the swinging sack. Catching her with his boot, Mack sent the dog sliding and spinning along the marble, Precious yelping blue murder.

Florence screamed some more from above.

A door slammed.

Balling up his sack, Levi made for freedom, waving for Mack to hurry.

It was the ornate clock on a pedestal that caught Mack's eye. Scooping it into his sack as he passed — only stopped a couple of seconds — he was following Levi out the door, stopped by the cocking sound of a pistol.

"Get your fucking hands up."

Bringing them up, Mack watched Levi dash out the servants' entrance, leap over the yew hedge. Gone. Mack slowly turned.

A light switched on, and Mack watched Quinn padding down the stairs in his johnnies, his back flap flapping, his service revolver in his hand. Mack let go of the sack, raising his hands all the way up, the clock breaking and tumbling out. Buying Levi time.

Florence stood at the top of the stairs, wrapped in a robe, her hair messed, Precious running up and prancing around her, yapping, then rushing back down the stairs, along the marble hall, snapping again at Mack's leg.

Mack flicked a kick, Quinn sticking the pistol in his face, saying, "Do it again, give me cause. Go on, do it."

Florence egged Quinn to just shoot the damned thief and be done with it, coming down, hugging herself in the robe, snatching the sack and staring in at the plunder, her broken Victorian mantle clock. Grabbing at Quinn's pistol, wanting to shoot Mack herself.

Precious snapped hold of Mack's ankle, shaking her head for a better grip. Mack winced and stood, taking the pain.

. . . CRIBS AND COWYARDS

IT HAD been a dumb plan. Cursing himself from the mansion all the way to Pearly's for letting his loathing turn him pea-brained, Levi was wondering again what the hell happened to Liam Preston.

Snapping open the baby Remington now, he checked its double load, descending Pearly's stairs, Woody playing shadow behind him. Could just step in and shoot for dead center. Should have done it the other day. Trouble was, Quinn Healey had Mack.

Tucking the gun in his pants, Levi flapped his shirt over top. He pushed back the parlor's curtain, Quinn sitting with his back to the wall, out of line with the window, his copper hat and Colt on the table.

Looking at ease, Quinn guessed there was a pistol under the shirt, Levi dropping into the chair opposite, hands in his lap. Quinn swiveled the Colt, the barrel pointing at Levi. Then grinning, lacing his fingers behind his head.

"Want to dance around," Levi said, "or you want to get straight to it?"

"If I left it to Florence, she'd have had your nephew castrated," Quinn said. "Likely do it herself."

"Yeah, she's the fiery sort," Levi said, the derringer in his hand, under the table, pushing down the barrel lock with his thumb.

"Gonna cut you a break." The lawman laid his hands on the table and leaned in. Did it like he had all day.

"How's that?"

"See, I got word the coolies are holding a cockfight down at Ragpicker's tonight."

"Nice for them."

"Yeah, hell of a thing. Taking a rooster, cutting off its comb and wattles, sticking iron gaffs on its spurs. Pitting one against another. Those boys throwing buckets of money down, betting one bird to rip up the other. Sporting folk, the Chinese, I'll give them that. Steeped in tradition."

"You getting to it?"

"You want it plain, huh?"

"Would be nice."

"You're going down and robbing the winner."

Levi took a moment, saying, "Man'd have to be crazy to go down there."

"Heard tales of plague, huh? Tell you, that's all horseshit. Stories to sell newspapers. 'Sides, you'll be robbing them, not eating them. But, you want, take along some sulphur. You can fumigate the whole lot."

Back in Quentin, Levi had got his hands on a copy of the *Daily Bee*, an article talking about the barbwire that city officials threw around Chinatown, California to Stockton, Broadway to Kearney. A hell of a sight. No Chinese allowed in or out. Suspicions of plague without a shred of proof.

"You want your nephew out or not?"

"I go down there, he comes with me."

"Half are hopheads, doped on their black smoke, the rest are half the size of real men."

"Still want him with me."

Looking out the window, Quinn said, "Take the half-breed. Man's got to be good for something. But any cut you give him comes out of your end."

"Red Tom? My end, huh?"

"We split it, fifty-fifty."

"Fifty-fifty's fine, but I'm taking Mack."

Quinn waited, then smacked his fist down, nearly got shot for it. "That thick head of yours slow receiving messages? You get the winnings, then you get Mack." Quinn touched his pistol. The snap of the derringer's hammer made him lift the hand.

Aching to shoot him, Levi eased the hammer back.

Getting to his feet, Quinn took his pistol with his left hand, easing it into his holster, saying, "Cockfight's back of the alley. Way I heard it, they start around dark." He reached in a pocket nice and easy, pulled out a hand-drawn map and set it down. "Say we meet at midnight — at your old place." He started to leave. "Oh, just one more thing . . ."

Levi looked at him.

"Florence wants her loot back. Every fucking fork and spoon."

. . . RAGPICKER'S ALLEY

COBBLESTONES LOOKED slick under the street lamps. The two men scuttled along the empty street: Kearney to Sacramento to Webb. Both in traditional dress, with hair in plaited queues falling from under tight-fitting caps, both in baggy pantaloons. Shadows cast along the ramshackle storefronts. Now and then the men were lost to shadows under the covered walkways. The older man was Jee Feng, carrying the pillowcase over a shoulder, stuffed full of his winnings, a goose gun under the other arm. Weary from the night's entertainment, Jee longed to climb into bed with his wife. Still, he stayed vigilant, protecting the biggest win of his life, Chinatown being no place for the careless.

His son Jim Kee cradled the bamboo crate housing the prize cock; the thing looking half-plucked and patched together with mismatched feathers. The bird deserved care and attention, some water and grain.

The ground shivered hard enough to rattle the cobble-stones like bones. A laundry's window shook in its frame, old man Feng two-stepping to get his balance, chalking it up to the quart of *jiu* he drank at the fights.

Tucking up close to a market stall, Levi Hayes and Red Tom kept to the shadows, nearly a block behind them. The smell of ripe melons hung around the stall.

The tremor shook some melons loose, rolling in front of them. It had Red Tom spooked, whispering, "Could be a sign . . . from some pissed-off Pomo god."

"Just a bit farther."

"Much as I want to spring Mack, maybe we better come back toward morning. Pomo magic's some powerful shit."

Levi kept on, leaving Red Tom to weigh the cash and rescuing a friend versus his Indian hoodoo. Cash and friend won out, and Red Tom hustled after Levi, scouring the doorways and alleys, looking for any kind of movement. The street was deserted, but the spooky feeling stayed with him: tales of tong wars, plagues and death in the streets. He'd never been down here in broad daylight, let alone at night.

Then he froze. A streetwalker climbed a ladder from a basement den, raven-haired, small for her twenty-odd years, a white cotton dress over a slim build. Red Tom hissed, and Levi slipped under an awning, ducking behind baskets of gourds.

Passing under a lamp, the girl called Leung crossed the street, thinking little of the tremor; they happened all the time. Zeroing in on the two men skulking under Chu's awning. One white, one Indian, down here for a good time, pockets full of dollars. Giving plenty of hip as she stepped, going for sultry, she stopped in front of the market, a chance to make up for the slow night, the locals more interested in fighting cocks than in their own.

Levi and Red Tom stepped out, the Fengs nearly out of sight two blocks away.

"Two bits a lookie," Leung said, sweeping her eyes over them. Smiling, dimples forming on her pretty face. The tall white had some years, but his looks likely earned him a woman in a bed now and then. The Indian looked like he slept alone. Smiling straight teeth, she came close and touched his sleeve.

Pulling his arm back, Red Tom told her to get lost, following Levi.

"Four bits a feelie," she said, keeping step, Red Tom showing the back of his hand, warning her.

"Dollar — do me." On his heels, she pecked at Red Tom's sleeve, saying, "Do me, only a dollar."

Red Tom threw his arm. The slap cracked in the night. "Get lost, you flea-bag. For a dollar I'll do myself."

Reeling back, Leung nearly came out of her shoes, tasting blood. The bastard hit her. Hard. Her voice became shrill, yelling at him.

Levi flattened against a storefront, the Fengs turning and looking back — a whore contending over her fee with some drunkard. Happened all the time, same as the tremors. Turning, old man Feng shouldered the goose gun and walked on, Jim Kee following.

Catching her, Red Tom tried clapping a hand over her mouth, giving a last warning.

Biting the hand got her slapped harder. Bleeding from nose and mouth, she backed off, rage clouding her features.

Feng turned again, watching the yelling streetgirl recross the street, her heels clicking on the cobblestones. He lost sight of the man she'd been fighting with. Fumbling with his ring of keys, he let his son into the store, Feng throwing the bolt behind them.

Staying to the shadows, Levi moved low along the store-fronts, Red Tom behind him. The light flicked on in Feng's window, allowing them a look past the calligraphy painted on the glass. A dingy butcher shop with smoked meat and fish hanging above a worktable. Butcher knives and cleavers stuck in a wooden block, blood-soaked aprons draped over a bucket, blowflies on both sides of the glass.

Sucking on his bleeding hand, Red Tom looked back, relieved the whore was gone. How long before the red spots, the bleeding under his skin, the killing fever?

Jim Kee stood at the butcher block in the center of the room, a bare bulb over his head, counting off the money, pulling fistfuls of it from the pillowcase, stacking and bundling the bills, passing them to the old man. Father and son grinning at each other. Crates penning other cocks lined a shelf. In one corner, a bamboo curtain covered a doorway leading to what Levi figured were living quarters.

•

JEE FENG leaned the goose gun on the wall and slid a bushel of pigs' feet aside, fished a pair of keys from behind a jug, hunched and unlocked a small door, the iron safe built into the wall. Tugging out a strongbox, he stuck a second key in the lock and flipped it open, getting busy setting the stacked bills inside, Jim Kee counting as he passed the bundles, the old man still delirious with their good fortune, already spending it in his mind. Enough here to get his family on a train and away from this godforsaken place, go somewhere they wouldn't be treated like roaches, somewhere they could own property, someplace that didn't have a Chinese Exclusion Act or an Asiatic Exclusion League. Away from the tongs that fed off their own. He was thinking maybe Mexico.

•

COUNTING THREE, Levi and Red Tom heaved at the door, and they burst in.

Jim Kee came around the butcher block, Red Tom's sap cracking across his skull, sending him stumbling back into the shelves, his world spinning, his arms windmilling, knocking slabs of hanging meat and crates of roosters, the birds squawking and flapping. As he reeled off the shelf, Red Tom cracked him a second blow, putting him down, feathers scattering through the air.

Slamming the strongbox shut, old man Jee grabbed for the goose gun, Levi rounding the table and catching hold of the barrel, leveling his own sap across the white head.

Laying the goose gun on the table, nudging Jee Feng with his foot, Levi opened the strongbox. "Mother of Jesus." He lifted out stacks of bills.

"Goddamn, motherlode," Red Tom said, sizing up the prize, forgetting about the plague and pissed-off gods.

Levi started piling the stacks into his satchel, keeping a count, one eye on the door.

"All this from fighting chickens," Red Tom said, summing a mental tally, stuffing the loose bills from the table into his own bag. Seven hundred. Eight. Eight-fifty. A thousand. "Jesus, there must be . . ." He lost count, did a little jig on the straw-strewn floor. No matter, he was one rich Pomo.

Nodding to the bamboo curtain, Levi told him to stop dancing and go check in back.

Throwing a salute, Red Tom took his pistol and satchel, sucking at his hand, going through the bamboo beads. Hoping he wasn't walking into an opium den, mistaking the smell of the incense.

No bodies lying comatose, stretched out on cribs. No pipes, brass needles or scrapers. No trays of cloisonne. No ancient crone on a mat tending a pipe, twisting a sticky glob on a pin over an opium lamp. Just nice rooms, small but clean. Modest furnishing. A woman asleep in the back bedroom. Pushing back through the bamboo, Red Tom watched Levi drop a couple bundles of cash next to the old man, asking, "What the hell you doing?"

"More than we need. Let's go," Levi said, taking the satchel's strap over a shoulder, moving for the door, stopping up short.

Grabbing the other bag, Red Tom bumped into him.

Four men stood fanned out, blocking the doorway, none of them small, stoned or old. Armed with long knives and cleavers. One holding a staff. The streetwalker stepped between the middle two, aiming a finger at Red Tom, throwing angry words in her native tongue.

"What the fuck's this, then?" Red Tom said, setting his satchel down between his feet, letting them see the pistol.

"Nothing good." Levi flapped his jacket back, hand over the derringer, sizing the men up.

Not the buck-toothed drunken Indian she described. The four men looked at each other for pluck, old man Feng and his son laid out inside their butcher shop.

The eldest, Shea, pointed with his knife, saying to Red Tom, "You touch Leung, you pay money."

The others nodded like it was only reasonable.

"Never touched the fleabag, just slapped sense in her, is

all," Red Tom said, holding up his hand, showing the crescent bite in the meat of his hand. "This look like I been pleasured, by Christ?" Pulling and cocking the pistol, he said, "Down in the Barbary, we shoot bitches for lots less."

Catching hold of Red Tom's sleeve, Levi guessed these weren't tong, the four more interested in restitution than in a fight. "No hand was laid on her, boys," Levi said, feeling inside his satchel, taking a stack of bills, tossing it on the ground.

All eyes on it.

"Enough there, maybe she'll give you a family discount," Red Tom said, eyes going from one man to the next. "Now, by Christ, step out of the fucking way." Red Tom thinking before Levi gave all the cash away.

Leung stooped for the money, came up waving the stack at Red Tom. "I no fleabag. You a asshole."

The one called Shea knew there was plenty more in the satchels, had been down at the cockfights, saw Feng have his big night. He sized these two up, the tiny gun in the tall one's hand, the Indian looking drunk enough to be slow with the pistol, the satchel between his feet. His brother Kim had the same idea, glanced at him and started swishing his cleaver, twirling it like a baton.

Leung waved the money at Red Tom, same time Kim moved and swung the blade, meaning to hack into him.

Jerking his head back, Red Tom snatched for the money waved in his face, Kim's cleaver striking the meat of Leung's arm, just above the wrist. Her mouth sprang into a big O, eyes on the cleaver stuck in her forearm. Red Tom let go of the money, Leung sinking to her knees, the cleaver in her arm, the bills fluttering from her fingers. Staring at blade and the blood, Leung's eyes rolled back, and she flopped down, her head striking the cobblestones. The cleaver clanged to the stones, blood spurting from the wound.

Not believing what he'd done, Kim held his head and ran off screaming.

"Ain't no good to no one now," Red Tom said, fanning his Colt between the other three.

Dropping the knife, Shea picked Leung up in his arms and hurried off, the last of the bills falling from her fingers.

Yow bent and picked up the bills, saying, "All for a lousy dollar." Fast with the staff, he whacked Red Tom's pistol away, swung it on the downstroke and caught him on the jaw, sent him reeling. Flipping the staff in both hands, Yow slammed it down on Levi's foot, then grabbed for Red Tom's satchel. Jumping at him, Red Tom grabbed hold of the staff and threw a fist, knocking Yow into the street. The man scrambled to his feet and hurried after Shea.

Hobbling a circle, Levi cursed at the pain, Red Tom slinging his satchel over his shoulder, looking around for the pistol, bending for it.

Stumbling to the door, young Jim Kee clapped a hand to his head, the butcher knife in the other, a light coming on across the street, faces appearing at windows. People yelling.

"Let's get gone." Levi limped double-time back the way they came.

Aiming the pistol, Red Tom chased Jim Kee back into the shop, the son slamming the door, screaming blue murder, trying to get to the goose gun. Smashing out the glass, Red Tom caught a handful of shirt and jerked Jim Kee back and halfway through the jagged glass, cracking him atop the head, Jim Kee's body going limp.

The fighting cocks kicked off in another bout of flapping,

more lights coming on up and down the block, folks gathering, shouting and pointing from doorways.

Leaving Jim Kee draped through the door, Red Tom started after Levi, waving his pistol for all eyes to see, yelling, "Ain't afraid to use it." Levi nearly out of sight.

Old man Feng got his feet under him, his world spinning, rocketing pain in his head. His fortune lost, his firstborn hanging through the door. Stumbling to the door, leveling the goose gun across Feng's back, he fired a volley up the street, his wife coming from the back, shrieking at him.

Red Tom felt the stinging shot in his arm, turned and fired back at Feng, faces disappearing from the doorways and windows.

Loading in another shell, Feng yelled for his wife to get down, raised the barrel and blasted another load. Firing high. Red Tom stood a few seconds longer, raised his arm steady, emptying his own pistol, blowing out the front window and butcher shop lights.

Feng pulled Jim Kee from the door, down to the floor, held his wife close, bullets tearing up his place. Feng wondering why the fuck he paid protection to the Hop Sings. The tong never there when he needed them.

Hurrying up the street, Red Tom held up the empty pistol, the satchel clutched tight, yelling he'd kill the next fucker for sure, looking up ahead for Levi.

. . . CHEAP SHOT

LEVI HOBBLED, Red Tom helping him up Stockton, over to
Battery. Looking behind, making sure they weren't followed,
they ducked into Corona Alley, back of a hardware. Red
Tom forced the back door, finding a railroad lantern inside,
Levi coming up with a kerosene can. Over at Pike's Place,
Red Tom talked the barman out of a bottle of Kentucky
straight in a Dr. Cumming's Cure-All quart, promising pay-
ment the next day. The two of them making the rest of the
way up the dark street, past the line of old brothels, going
into the House of Blazes. Levi scraping a match to light
their way inside.

Dragging off his boot while Red Tom poured the kerosene in the filler, Levi perched on one of the casks. Red
Tom struck a match, raised the glass, got the lantern going,
adjusting the wick. Testing the drink.

Giving his foot a look, wiggling the toes, Levi figured no
bones were broken. The swelling told him it could stand a

soaking in salts when he got back to Pearly's; hell, his whole body could use a soaking in salts. The Barbary taking its toll on him.

The lantern cast light on the heap of bills Levi counted out, stacking it on the second cask. Quinn's share. The cask was filled with the loot Levi had taken from the Healey mansion. The satchel with the rest of the cockfight money was tucked under the straw of the cask Levi perched on. Red Tom kept testing the whiskey, eyeing the stack of bills, thinking about the money Levi had already lost to the Chinese, tipping the quart, splashing some on the bitten hand, Levi telling him he'd be fine, adding, "Might want to get Pearly to dig out that shot though." Pointing at his shoulder.

Flinching at the thought of that heavy-handed woman digging around, Tom figured to let it heal on its own, saying, "Just want to be around long enough to spend my share." Looking at the stacked bills, tipping the bottle again. "Gets me in a stew, that heathen biting her teeth in me." Showing the crescent bite-mark again, going on about plague and how the Chinese woman got what was coming.

"You're one durable son," Levi said. "Still, I were you, I'd get that shot dug out."

"Alright, Mother, I'll get it tended." Red Tom offered the bottle. Levi waving it off, just wanting this over, Mack released from whatever jail Quinn had him in.

"Stews me, too, you giving away money like that, my money," Red Tom said. "And just how much we giving up this time?"

"Couple hundred should do it," Levi said. "He'll be expecting least that."

"We fight half of Chinatown, get shot up and stomped and bit, and that fucker gets half."

"On account Mack's in his jail."

"Sure would be nice to watch that fat son cross the great divide."

"Can't argue that," Levi said, thinking it would happen soon enough.

A creaking board had them turning, Quinn walking in, moving into the light, pistol in his hand. "Nice, you boys are sentimental about this place," he said, looking around the dark, the top of the stairs, behind the bar, stepping past the open trapdoor. "Shacktown, we call it now."

"Call it what you like," Levi said, pointing to the money.

Sucking from his bottle, Red Tom swallowed his contempt, tempted to draw and be done with it, shove the fat man down that hole by the bar, take their chances on finding the jail holding Mack and busting him out.

Quinn's eyes fell on the money. He stepped to it, still cautious, half-expecting an ambush.

"We do all the work, and you get half the pay," Red Tom said.

Picking up the stack, Quinn rifled the bills, seeing the blood on Red Tom's sleeve, saying, "Didn't just hand it to you, huh?"

"Not like we're handing it to you," Red Tom said.

"You got your share, so, let's go get Mack," Levi said, wishing Red Tom would shut up.

Tucking away the bills, Quinn said, "Soon's we settle the matter of bail."

Red Tom sputtered, whiskey coming out his nose.

"Another hundred sounds right," Quinn said, looking at his pistol like he was admiring it.

"That kind of joking ain't healthy," Red Tom said, tossing the empty quart and squaring up.

"'Less I miss my guess, you boys miscounted the split by at least that much." Quinn's eyes stayed on Red Tom, the man wobbling and stepping to the wall, unbuttoning his britches.

"Maggoty piece of crook with a badge." Red Tom unslung his belt, hand on the pistol to keep it from dropping.

"About all I'm going to hear, breed." Quinn wagging his pistol at the man's back. "And you don't need that pistol for pissing. Toss it down, and do it easy."

"I'm tending my business right now, and for me that takes two hands."

Aiming at Red Tom, Quinn glanced at Levi.

Levi hadn't moved.

"Toss it or you'll be leaking out a new hole."

Shrugging, Red Tom eased the pistol out, stayed facing the wall, his britches sliding halfway down. "For fuck's sakes, now, you got me pissing on myself. Maybe you got more 'n one pair, but I only got the one." That's when he spun and fired, his shot just high and wide.

Quinn fired back and hit Red Tom square, wheeling on Levi before he could pull the derringer.

Pitched to the straw, Red Tom lay there, looking up at the pigeons flying about the rafters.

Half-off the cask, Levi froze, knowing Quinn had him. No chance of fanning the hammers. He watched Red Tom turn his head, trying to speak, then tipping back on the wet straw.

"Calls for a change of plans," Quinn said, motioning for him to drop it.

Levi set the derringer on the cask, the smell of powder, the ringing in his ears. Tom was down on the straw. No telling how bad he was hit.

Stepping close, Quinn took the derringer with his left hand, looked at it, went over and fired both barrels into Red Tom, tossing it at Levi's feet. "There you go. One less drunk breed. Some folks might call that a service to the community." Stepping back to Levi. "Way it looks to me, you boys were drinking, likely got in an argument over ill-gotten gains when I came by, drawn by your light. Heard the shots and came in too late to stop proceedings. Just managed to get the better of you . . . again." He smiled. "Now, of course, if you were to tell where you hid the gold . . ."

Levi glared at him.

"Didn't think so," Quinn said, flipping the Colt, swinging it by the barrel, catching Levi on the temple, watching him fall, knocking over the cask, the lid rolling off, loot from Florence's spilling from the sack. Taking the lantern, putting his boot on the other cask, he tipped it over, the satchels rolling out.

Holstering, Quinn stooped and counted the bundles of cash, saying, "Your nephew's gonna do time, but you, my friend, are ripe to hang."

Prodding Levi with a shoe, he scooped Florence's stuff back in the sack. Righting the casks, he figured it was a good a place as any, dropping the satchels back in, scattering in handfuls of straw, leaving the lids off, looking natural. The only people who knew it was here were dead or fucked.

He flipped Levi with his shoe, snapped the handcuffs on his wrists. He'd throw him in the cell with his nephew, the old jail down off Castro, used as an overflow drunk tank, just one old fossil named Dingwall on night duty, far enough from Quinn's higher-ups and official eyes.

Still a decent hour, he'd head back up to Nob Hill afterwards and pay a call on Florence, give her back her junk, feign concern about the sailor that had been hanging around. Tend to unfinished business while Marvin was off at sea — the business these crooked assholes had interrupted.

He'd come back for the money in the morning, head over and grease Judge Meade's palm over breakfast of ham and eggs at the Palace, buy himself a hanging verdict, a sure way of steering clear of getting gut-shot from a Barbary window while walking his beat some night. Still, his thoughts were on the gold coins, Quinn looking around, thinking where Hayes might have hid them. He'd been all through this place, top to bottom. A dozen times and nothing. He'd give Hayes one more crack at buying back the hanging verdict with the coins.

Then he was thinking about Florence again. God, what that woman could do to a man.

... SYDNEY TOWN

THE DREAM started the same way, Levi floating over the American River and topping a bluff, the sawmill beyond the tips of the dogwoods. Pap panning in the tailrace, Levi catching the glint of placer gold in the pan. Then the two of them were dancing in the stream.

Light from a street lamp crept in, somebody calling his name, the dream fading. Felt like a knob above his temple, caked blood in his hair. That awful throbbing, Levi trying to crawl back into that dream.

The cell reeked of the detained and unwashed, strong enough to turn any man's stomach. Wishing now that things had worked out with Minnie Baker, the girl he met after getting out of Quentin, thinking he should have gone to work on her daddy's sheep farm, headed up to Seattle. Thinking he would've seen indoor plumbing for himself.

"You back with us?" Mack sat on the opposite iron bunk, elbows on his knees, looking at Levi. His bowler gone.

"Idea was to get you out," Levi said, pressing himself up and looking around, getting a sense of where he was. The smell of sheep had to beat the smell in this place.

"Another plan not working out."

"Yeah, well . . . got any water in this place?"

"This look like the Fairmont?" Mack rubbed the stubble on his chin. "That fucker Quinn's talking about a hanging."

"Yeah, the man likes to talk."

"Says he's off first thing to buy the verdict."

"He tell you about Red Tom?"

"Said you shot Tom while gunning for him." Mack leaned against the stone, looking over.

"You believe that?"

"Know you're too good a shot," Mack said.

The scrape of a key in a lock, and the outer door swung open, Quinn standing with a bucket of water and a ladle, grinning.

"Remember the first time you come to the Blazes," Levi said to him, figuring the man could only hang him once.

"That right?"

Levi looked to Mack. "Quinn brung his long arm of the law and ran smack into Nikko." Turning back to Quinn. "Remember that? Tossed you and two of your finest out on your asses, one after the other, hats, guns and uniforms stripped off them and nailed over the bar." Memories worth hanging for.

Nothing was changing Quinn's mood. He smiled, saying, "Got a better story. One with you about to hang."

"Yeah," Levi looked to Mack, saying, "old Quinn and his law boys sure beat a retreat that day, all the way down to Market, folks watching them running in their johnnies."

Not in the mood, Mack came off his bunk and went to

the small window, wishing he could squeeze through the bars, thinking if his uncle kept talking, they were more likely to dangle from the gibbet without ever seeing a judge.

Levi swung his feet to the floor, one boot on, one boot gone, stepping to Quinn, the bars between them, staring into the man's eyes.

"More than one imbecile's dangled from your family tree," Quinn said, looking back, ladling water. "Pity you, going up in front of Judge Meade, gavel in one hand, rope in the other. You remember Meade, same one sent you to Quentin." He drank, saying, "That time cost Marvin a hundred. This time'll be more. Cost of things these days." Pouring the water back in the bucket, he glanced at his timepiece. "Three hours from now, with no Nikko in sight." Quinn ladled more of the water and poured it on the floor, saying, "'Bout the same time I fetch the money you hid in that barrel."

Levi gripped his fists on the bars. "I hang and you won't be seeing those coins."

"Going to put my money in the Mercantile, except what I got to pay Meade." Quinn dropped the ladle back in the bucket. "So you know, it's your share's paying for it. Paying for breakfast at the Palace, too."

"Go on and fuck yourself."

"Hear Meade likes the way the cook does his eggs." Quinn rattled his keys. "I come back and you tell what you did with the coins, maybe we can work something out." Levi Hayes wanting the deed back meant the coins had to be hidden in that fucking place where he shot the Indian, the House of Blazes. Quinn saying as he left, "You got till morning . . ."

. . . AVENGING ANGEL

The knock stopped Florence mid-thrust.

Underneath her, Van Doy propped himself up on an elbow, saying, "Who calls past midnight?"

Climbing off him, she threw on her robe and went to the window. Couldn't see a thing. "You close the gate?"

"Same as always."

She knew who it was. Quinn, knowing she was home alone — Marvin supposedly on the *Star of Bengal* — coming to finish what they started. Could be fun, these two running into each other.

Tying the sash, she told Van Doy to keep still, let herself out and went down the stairs, Precious running ahead, growling. Quinn's thoughts likely carnal, but it could be Marvin's body had washed up; she'd left the disposal to halfwits. The knock came again. She stood at the bottom of the stairs in the dark, deciding the best play.

Tousling her hair and rubbing her eyes, she swung the door back. "Quinn!" She went into his arms.

"Sorry, had to climb your —" Quinn caught her, bringing her back inside, flicking the door closed with his foot, easing her to the bottom stair, setting down the sack of loot. "You alright, Flo?"

She slumped into him, put her arms around his neck. Sobbing against his chest, saying, "I should've told you . . . said something before."

Looking down the long hall and up the stairs. "You alone?"

"Uh huh." Tears rolled down, Florence pressed into him.

He ran a hand over her black hair, the moonlight coming through the window tinging it blue. Her body warm in his arms, the sweet smell of her, holding her close, feeling her shudder. "Should've told me what?"

Whatever doleful mood she was in, he'd get her past it, show his intentions. Marvin was no match for her, that much was plain. The son of a bitch hitting her.

"And I would have," she said, pulling back and putting a hand to her chest, "oh, my heart's in my throat, the way those men . . ."

"What men?" She wasn't making sense, Quinn confused by his own agenda.

"Promised foul play if I uttered a word." Nuzzling her head against his shoulder, she let herself tremble, puffing against his neck, Precious whimpering and running circles in the foyer.

"Slow down now, Flo. From the beginning, please." Stroking her hair. God, she was magnificent. "Let me get you some water."

"Brandy." Nicking her head to the trolley in the parlor.

Going to a lamp, he fumbled for the pull chain, found a

shot glass on the trolley and poured, brought it to her and watched her sink it in a swallow. He had to go back for another, brought the bottle.

"I wanted to tell you . . . would have . . ." She tipped the bottle, followed with a shudder and sob.

Wiping her tears with his thumbs, being gentle about it, Quinn forgot the sack of loot he came to return, asking again, "What men? Marvin's men?"

Handing him the bottle, she shook her head, turning her head to the banister. Quinn put an arm around her, sitting next to her, giving her time. "Did he hit you again, that son of a bitch?"

"Wish he were here to do it," Florence said. "Practically welcome it." Turning to him, sinking down, her arms around his waist, head in his lap.

"Can't help if you don't tell me?"

Coming up, eyes streaming tears, Florence thinking this was child's play, she said, "You're right, Quinn." She righted herself, collecting herself. "The two men . . ."

"Hayes?"

She nodded. "Came here demanding to see Marvin. Couple nights before they robbed me."

Quinn let her go and rose.

"Marvin showed them into the study. I knew something was wrong, but, uh, the way they were quarreling through the door, over some deed or other."

Quinn putting it together. Smiling. Hayes and Lewis right in his cell.

"He left with them in the pitch, and he's not been back." She clung to the railing, telling herself not to overplay it.

"You should've . . ."

"I know."

Her wet eyes searched his, Florence pretending not to notice the excitement he couldn't hide. Brushing against him. "Oh, Quinn, I don't think Marvin's on the *Star of Bengal* at all. Think something's happened."

"I'll find out." Could be a miracle. Marvin could be dead. He'd send Dingwall, the night jailer, home early, inflict enough pain upon the nephew, pound a nail into a knee, scrape the bone, let him scream, make Hayes watch, make him give up the coins. Then they'd hang. Better yet, they'd try to escape, both gunned down in the attempt. Save himself paying for Meade's verdict. He kissed her forehead, saying, "I'll make it right, Flo."

She nodded, pulled herself together.

Quinn knew how he'd play this. He'd have the gold, would have the woman, too.

There was no paperwork on Hayes and Lewis having been taken to the old holding facility down off Castro— and just old Dingwall on duty. The city holding most prisoners of record at the Hall of Justice or over at Broadway, both up in North Beach, the Castro jail just used in times of overflow now. If anybody found out, Quinn could say he dragged them there for interrogation.

He'd leave his horse here. Could be he'd need an alibi. He'd borrow another one or maybe an auto, make his way across town and get it out of them. Could just shoot them through the barred window — justice being swift. Rough part of town, and these two would have enemies, Quinn thinking of the line of men up by St. Anthony's Mission. Not hard to sell, with Hayes just released from Quentin. He'd work it out on his way down there.

Then he'd make his way back here, comfort the widow, establish the alibi.

. . . JAILBREAK

THE CITY slept. The foreshock rocked the ground, a low growl rising from it, the jolt worse than the tremors of the past few days.

Snapping awake, Mack felt the floor seesaw. Dust shaking from the ceiling. He coughed and stumbled, trying to see past the bars.

"It'll pass," Levi said, covering his mouth and nose, facing the dank wall, pain intense from the knock to the head.

Hands on the bars, Mack gasped for air, only able to see half a block in either direction. Just silhouettes of low-level buildings, one stacked against the next. Had no idea where they were. Couldn't see much when Quinn first brought him in, tied up and lying on the floor in the back of the cart. Pretty sure it wasn't the jail on Market. Nothing out there familiar. Looked like the outskirts.

A wagon rolled up the middle of the street, a produce dealer making his rounds, sitting hunched with his collar turned up, hat low, warding off the creeping chill of morning. The man spoke to his mule, trying to ease her on account of the tremor. The mule's hooves clip-clopped on the cobblestone, echoing in the stillness. Stopping at the corner, the mule relieved itself, splashing the stones.

The figure of a man hopped off the back of the wagon, bounding over the splash, a storm in his stride, angling for the station, not a word to the dealer shaking the reins and clucking at the mule.

"Christ," Mack said, seeing the figure coming, stepping back.

"Told you, it'll pass."

"We got Quinn coming." The look of the man sent a chill, Mack forgetting the foreshock, snapping his fingers to get Levi up.

The ground gave another rumble, more dust shaking down. Somewhere a door slammed.

. . . 5:12

HUNCHED AT the side of her bed, hand on the bedpost, Van Doy tried fixing his eyes on his feet in the dark. Bathed in sweat, he was out-waiting the stitch in his side, felt like a hot poker going through his ribs. Deep breathing doing nothing for it. The first chirps of birds foretold the arrival of morning. This woman's oyster had a hunger. Damned thing was killing him. Had to be the hysteria, this woman having a bad case.

Cuddled in her sheets, hands on her knees, Florence rocked back and forth, humming "Mandy Lee," reveling in her widowhood. Van Doy had risen to the occasion — four times this night, twice since Quinn had gone. Florence smiling, feeling a fifth one on its way.

Precious whimpered in her basket next to the bed, feelings of neglect.

"What's goddamn wrong now, Precious?" Florence tired

of the incessant whine, thinking she ought to give the dog to the Spanish maid.

"Suppose he'll come back?" Van Doy asked, thinking he was in no condition for facing Quinn.

"Oh, Van, I gave that boy plenty to occupy his mind, trust me. Guarantee he won't be back any time soon." She could lose her patience with this ape, putting the sweetness in her voice, saying, "Come on now, sugar, it's near morning. Come comfort your Flo, then you can catch your wink while I have the girl fix you coffee and eggs."

"Not afraid of that copper. Hope you're not thinking it." Laying his head on the pillow next to her, he sighed, the woman's hand on him, working him like a churn.

"Never thought it."

"Telling a man to hide in the closet . . ."

"I wouldn't call what you did hiding. Playing it smart, is how it was." Van Doy in her armoire when she rid herself of Quinn. Found him there when she came back to bed, Van Doy saying he was sure she told him to hide in there. Hand working under the sheet, she said, "Let's just rid your mind of such trifles."

Good as it was going to get. Swinging a leg over him, she got on top. Hurling a pillow at the whimpering dog, Precious scurrying under the bed. "There now, forget the dog, forget Quinn, and forget the time. It's just me and you." She pushed him in. "Promise you, Quinn comes back, you can shoot him all you want."

The deep rumble rocked the house, slowed, then rocked again, felt like a ship in a gale. The floor jerked, the bed sliding across the room, and Florence was pitched naked from the bed. Chunks of plaster struck her like hail. Arms over her head, she staggered around, trying to call for Van Doy. Choking on the dust. Hearing him gag.

A crack sketched across the ceiling, more plaster rained down, the chandelier swinging on its chain, the windows blown out. The bed slid into her, knocking Florence down screaming.

Van Doy tried to climb into his trousers, hopping through the shaking, calling for her, coughing plaster dust, the massive armoire toppling onto him.

. . . ALL HELL'S LOOSE

SMUT ROSE, blocking the light filtering through the bars. Next jolt came harder, the dry chalkiness filling his throat, stinging his eyes, Levi trying to spit. Shielding his face, he felt around the blackness, trying to call for Mack. Mack trying to call back, both stumbling around, the floor shaking, turning to rubble.

Levi got against the wall, his shirttail over his face. Felt like a hell of a force was throttling the jail by the neck, the floor rising, the concrete crumbling underfoot.

•

CHARGING THROUGH the outer door, Quinn was bounced from wall to wall, stumbling down the hall, felt like the place was disintegrating, doing what he could to stay on his feet, intent on getting to his prisoners. Couldn't yell out. The ceiling caved in, lath and boards crashing down, knocking him to the floor, cutting him and coating him in grey.

Getting up. Hand over his mouth and nose. The power was lost, everything black. A beam crashed next to him.

Feeling his way along the broken wall, he found the outer door to the cell. Jammed and knocked out of plumb. Squeezing through an opening in the smashed wall, he drew his pistol, cocking it, eyes burning, trying to breathe, searching for an outline, any hint of a target.

The next shudder pitched him down, something sharp striking his back, the pistol jarred from his hand. Fighting to stay conscious, Quinn got to his knees, gagging and clawing around for the Colt.

So much dust he couldn't breathe. Patting around, he found the pistol again, gagging, pulling himself to his feet. The rear wall spilled into the hall, filling it with broken shingles and boards. Up to his knees in it. Pulling himself free.

A shadow moved to his left, a shaft of light giving him a target. Firing two rounds — trying to keep his shots low, aiming for the belly — he heard a cry, saw the shape of a man go down. Moving to it, he tripped into a smashed desk, nails stabbing his thigh. Finding the body, Quinn felt and searched for a pulse. The man was dead, but he couldn't tell if it was Hayes or Lewis, then his hand found the badge pinned to the jacket. The head buried under plaster and board.

Fuck.

Getting up, he heard the roof groan; stumbling and needing to find a way out, needing air, looking for any ghost of movement.

•

Levi and Mack were thrown clear, the cell wall tumbling into the street. Holding the bars as the outer wall collapsed, Levi ended up lying among the busted brick and masonry. Able to breathe again, he got up and found Mack, covered in grey, looking like an ancient man.

A fissure ripped up the street, the ground around it turning to a rolling sea, cobblestones dancing like corn in a popper. The sidewalk heaved and snapped. The earth grumbled, and a row of power poles swayed like a line of drunks.

Somewhere, a church bell clanged like it had gone mad. Across from the jail, a livery wall caved in, its stoop spilling in the street. A woman shrieked.

No telling where the shot came from, Levi turned, seeing the shape of a man inside the ruin, the man white with dust. The main support running the length of the jail gave way, and the roof thundered down, burying the man. Levi hoping it was Quinn.

Hands on each other, the two of them looked around as a telegraph office across the way collapsed, Levi tugging Mack to the middle of the street. No idea where they were. Trying to get his bearings, he led Mack by the arm. Could be Castro from the look of it, the buildings low and sparse.

"Busted out by the good Lord himself," Mack said, spitting grit, snorting to clear his nose. A cut showed across his forehead; he felt the wet of the blood.

"If that's the good Lord, He's mighty boiled about some shit or other." Levi quickened his step, tugging Mack along, looking over his shoulder, trusting Quinn lay crushed under the mangled jail house. If there was a God, Levi hoped He got that part right.

A chunk of brick tore into his bare foot, same foot the

Chinese man smashed with his staff, Levi hopping to the new pain. He looked at his feet, one boot on, one boot lost. Somewhere back there.

.... WHISPERS TO SCREAMS

THE STATION's framework stuck up like the bones of a carcass, Quinn worming from under the lath and shingles,
pressing with his back, coughing up what he hadn't swallowed, mouth and tongue coated with it. Spitting. Steadying
himself in the wreckage, he tried making sense of things —
a massive quake, like nothing he'd ever felt before. Looked
like the world had gone down around him.

No sign of Levi Hayes or his nephew, townsfolk flocking
into the street. A state of fear and confusion.

Flipping open the cylinder, he shoved in fresh shells,
dropping a couple, his eyes searching the street. The walls
of the telegraph next door looked set to buckle, its support
beams fractured. It gave a sway, then fell into the street,
people jumping out of the way.

. . . DOWN IN THE MISSION

THE GLIMMER of dawn, a quake that lasted bare minutes, with bedlam following behind. The first of the flames showed above what Levi guessed were the rooftops of the Mission District.

First thought was to head south, get away from the tall buildings. He watched townsfolk gather in front of the wrecked telegraph. Bewildered and panicked, more of them spilled into the street, nobody sure which way to go, fingers pointing at the flames starting to show across the rooftops.

Levi figured Quinn had gone back to see the grieving widow — him and Mack interrupting things when they robbed the place — the woman staging her theatrics, letting Quinn know Marvin met his end. Spinning her version, how Levi and Mack helped him to meet it. Quinn dumb enough to believe it, coming back here to avenge things, have a turkey shoot in his holding cell, the quake spoiling his plans.

With any luck, the fucker was dead under the tonnage of police station walls. Joining his brother. If he wasn't, Levi and Mack needed to get out of there.

The ground quivered like pudding, another low rumble, a supply store's facade dropped into the street; a man and woman carrying bundles were buried. Folks rushed in, pulling them out, laying them in the street and crowding around.

Porch beams dropped ahead of a man leading a mule, the panicked animal rearing and kicking, breaking its tether and running toward the Mission. Taking hold of Mack's sleeve, Levi pulled him out of its path.

"Where the hell to?"

"We go get our gold," Levi said, looking toward the tall silhouettes of the city.

A water main burst, a geyser shooting higher than the rooftops, showering down. Pulling tight to a place called Griffin's, they bumped the man stepping from his door, his apron on, hand to his forehead, blood dripping from a gash. Tugging up his suspenders, the fellow, Griffin, said he wasn't believing what he was seeing. The force of the gushing water snapped his sign from its chains. Dropped next to him. Kicking at it, he looked at the blood on his hand, turned back inside, calling for his wife.

Levi searched the faces of those wandering the street, looking for Quinn. Thinking it through. Get to the gold plastered into the cellar. That and the money Quinn left in the casks, and get out of town. "Any idea where the hell we're at?"

"Thinking that might've been the Dolores station," Mack said, looking back. "Caught sight of the top of City Hall, but couldn't tell how far he brung me, tied and on the floor in back of some cart." The cart had smelled of rot under the tarp, not a proper jail wagon, that was for sure. Stepping over a corbel lying in pieces, ash floating on the air. Swiping a hand, Mack flicked embers from his hair, following Levi.

Electric poles running the length of the street leaned this way and that, power lines undulating like skipping ropes. Bricks and broken glass scattered everywhere, the wall of a bakery strewn across the sidewalk. A sign reading *home-made pies* lay in the rubble. The shop's window was smashed out, its door hanging open. The interior remained as it was, shelves of bread and cakes and pastries on display in their cases, dust and glass blanketing everything like icing.

Levi led the way; they'd keep to the side streets, in case Quinn dodged the devil and was out there, Levi knowing he'd come after them. Best thing was to head over to Stockton, then west. Get what was his and get out of there.

. . . UP IN SMOKE

SPIKES BIT like teeth. Quinn moved, feeling the thunderbolt shoot up his arm. Clutching it tight, he grimaced, knowing it was broken above the wrist. His hand dangled, useless. Needed to be splinted and wrapped, but right now all he could do was tuck it close. Ignore the pain.

Shoving the pistol into the crook of the arm, he loaded in the last shell with his good hand. No telling how wide the quake hit, no sign of his prisoners, but he knew where they'd go. He'd take Castro to Market. The badge and gun lending him speed.

No sign of Dingwall, the duty officer. Pretty sure it was him he shot in the outer cell. He'd hang it on Hayes and Lewis, say they killed the officer making their break.

Milling in the street, people stood in hollow-eyed panic, not sure which way to go. A couple of livery men led a draught team through the crowd, adding to the confusion. A crack and rumble from an exploding gas main sounded from over in the Mission, spooking the horses, sending them rearing, shaking their great heads. People closest were knocked down, the livery men trying to control the beasts.

Quinn started moving, eyes sharp for his prisoners.

. . . UNDER A FALLING SKY

IN NIGHT clothes, his feet stamped into slippers, Milton Porter led his wife, Mabel, into their street. He draped his frock about her shoulders, the only thing he had grabbed as they ran outside. Mabel holding their child, closing the garment around her, warding the dust and morning chill. Wiping his specs, Milton told her the worst was over, the middle of the street being the safest place.

Attendants ushered youngsters from the Booth Home for Children at the far end of the block, the matron calling, asking what that was.

Milton calling back, "God's wrath." Fearing an after-shock, he pointed her over to the vacant lot, telling her, "Assemble the children there."

Everything they owned was inside the apartment house, their top-floor flat. Just had it wallpapered. Not wanting to leave his wife and child in the street, Milton said, "I'm going back," thinking he'd cram what he could in a coffer. Jewelry, cash, stock certificates, something for the baby. If the garage was standing, he'd get the Runabout and drive them out of town; maybe Oakland had gone unscathed. They'd wait it out like any storm. He started moving, seeing the two men coming up the street.

•

THE SIDE street was Java. Coming from its south end, Mack pegged the blonde woman, the one from out front of the St. Anthony's Mission two days back, her hair hanging long this time. He recognized the husband, too, the man starting to walk away from her. Mack called to her, asking if she was alright.

"I'm not decent, sir," Mabel said, standing in the street in her nightdress and flimsy slippers, looking fearful, her hand rubbing the infant's back, looking to her husband, not liking the idea of him wanting to leave her out here half-dressed.

Mack saying they were the ones who'd intervened out front of St. Anthony's, Milton nodding his impatience, stepping back and looking to his four-story, saying, "Yes, yes, I remember, and I thank you for what you did," not sure he could trust them, hurrying his words, "and I'd be thanking you again if you watch over my wife and child for a minute. I've got things to tend." Pointing again to his four-story, he snugged the frock around wife and child, turning from her protests, not waiting on an answer. "I'll be but a wink."

Calling after him, Mabel glanced at the two men, then over at the orphans lining the vacant lot, the attendants doing a head count.

Another tremor rocked the ground.

Milton was running, hopping past fragments in the street, calling back he'd pay them for their trouble, ride them to safety. Ignoring his tenants out front of the building, asking him what was going on.

"Jesus Christ." Levi thinking he could have picked a better street, turning to the woman holding her baby. "Afraid we have some urgency, ma'am." He pointed to the orphans all holding hands now. "Best if you go stand with them; or, you like, you can come along, and your man can catch up in his auto."

"I'll stay put," she said. "Go if you want, I'm far from helpless, sir."

"Sure of that, ma'am," Levi said, nodding to Mack. "Let's go."

"Can't just leave her standing out here," Mack said, this woman in her nightdress, clutching the child.

"Woman's far from helpless. Just told you so."

"You notice she's got a kid?"

Levi pointed to the line of orphans.

The ground shook again, short, but abrupt. Children cried out, the attendants soothing them.

Milton took the steps to his front door, the name *Marathon* in script on the transom's window. An electric pole slumped out front, power lines tightening and snapping overhead, dropping to the sidewalk, writhing like vipers, hissing electricity, sparks shooting in all directions.

Knocked back to the walk, Milton regained his footing, dancing clear of one wire, jumping over the second like he was playing some child's game. Tenants calling for him to get away.

A crumbling chunk of pediment dropped from the rooftop, striking him, knocking him into the sparking lines. Milton's body jerked, then dropped between the lines, one of the tenants rushing to get to him, the snaking lines keeping the man back.

Screaming in wide-eyed horror, Mabel tried running to him, Mack catching her and turning her away. The woman twisting against his grip, the baby wailing.

"You can't go there," Mack said, holding her out by the arms, trying to reason.

Her kick was sharp. Mack giving her a shake. The woman clung to her screaming child, head turned to her man down on the sidewalk, yelling for Mack to let go. Mack looking to Levi, holding her fast. Nothing anyone could do.

The man was dead, Levi was certain of it. And if Quinn was living, they were in danger. Out here unarmed. Quinn was likely to go straight for the money, looking out for them as he went, set to shoot them down. The reason why Levi had picked the side streets.

Mabel kicked at Mack again, wanting to run to Milton.

Fires glowed orange in the distance, a kind of halo over the dark building tops. Not a light on anywhere. Plumes of smoke rolled in the distance like storm clouds, blocking the rising sun.

"Take a good look." Levi pointed, getting Mack to look at the spreading fire, meaning they didn't have much time. Levi called for the attendants to usher the orphans along, showing them the glow in the sky to the southeast. Some of the children were crying, aware what had happened to the man.

"We can't just leave Milton, not in the street," Mabel said, twisting to free herself of Mack's hold, trying to get to her husband.

"Only thing living's them goddamn wires," Mack said. "You want to lay the baby alongside your man?"

That stopped her, Mabel giving in to her sobbing, not believing Milton was dead. All of it happening too fast.

"Now, I'm sorry . . ." Mack looking from her to Levi.

Against any horse sense, Levi hurried to where Milton lay, confirming what was certain in his mind, careful of the lines, still sparking but hardly coiling now. The smell of burned flesh, one of Milton's hands fried black, his fingers gone, his hair singed away. One of the tenants asking Levi the state of the man, lowering his voice, asking how something like this might affect the rents.

Mabel cried, Levi hurrying back, shaking his head, saying he was real sorry, "Just nothing more can be done."

"Buck up, now, ma'am," Mack said, rubbing a hand on her back. "You got to be a brick now." He pointed to the glowing orange. "Know what that is? What it means?"

She looked and nodded.

He let her go, hands at her elbows to catch her if she bolted again. "Got to do it for your young one."

Sniffing, she pushed at the tears on her cheeks, letting him guide her along, patting the baby's back.

Feeling like he needed to say something more, Levi lied, saying, "Doesn't seem your man suffered. Happened quick."

They made their way along State, the attendants and orphans following. The day crew at the brickyard came to help with the orphans, taking them over by a shed, said they had water and a wagon coming. Levi wanting to leave Mabel and the baby with them, saying it was for the best, Mack saying no. "Woman's in no condition . . ."

Levi just started walking, muttering, Mack following, leading Mabel Porter and her child over to Castro.

In various stages of undress, a milling crowd moved in a like direction, heading toward the waterfront, most of them calm. Most in shock. The smell of smoke and the crackling roar from the growing fire pushed at their backs.

Some lined the street and watched it come, unable to leave everything they owned, not believing what was happening. One ancient man, dressed from the waist up, faltered and looked heavenward, hands held in prayer, calling to the Almighty to have mercy on their souls. His absent eyes fell on the two men and woman with the child. He declared it a conflagration and no place to be, then trotted along, moving into the crowd. A couple of boys found humor in the half-dressed man, pointing at him naked like that.

More flames showed bright above the flats up ahead, another glow over the building tops to the west. A fire of some size. Levi feeling like they were heading down a funnel.

The crowd kept at a steady pace, more joining all the time, some carrying belongings, some holding onto loved ones, some helping with the injured. All aiming for the Depot, moving like a stream.

"We get to the water, what then?" someone called.

Someone calling back, "Then we swim if we got to."

"We'll be fine," Mack said to Mabel, pulling the frock up, keep it from falling, noting the slippers on her feet. "We'll see you to safety, ma'am. You can count on that."

She nodded.

Mack followed Levi, not sure it was the way to go. It seemed they were walking in a line with the fire. And his uncle's luck hadn't been something to count on, and no one needed to remind him Quinn might be out there. Mack guessing the man would shoot them both on sight.

•

THE TWO women came from the flat above Grant's Upholstery, down a broken set of stairs, staid-looking and tramping into the torn road, one gripping an ironing board, the other an empty bird cage, the bottom tray missing. A hat of ostrich plumes pulled low over her eyes, she walked straight into Levi.

"Careful there, ma'am." Catching her from falling.

"Sakes alive, seems I've lost my Jimmy," Bird Cage proclaimed, peeking out from under the brim, her mouth trembling, eyes darting about like she was in shock.

"Appears so, ma'am." Levi tipped the hat from her eyes, pointing her up Market, saying, "Just keep heading straight up."

"He's a canary, you know, all yellow," she told him, walking along.

"I'll keep an eye peeled," Levi said, figuring she might have taken a knock, saying to her companion, "You ladies stay to the middle, and keep away from anything that might come down."

Ironing Board nodded.

"Goes by Jimmy," Bird Cage repeated, "my canary."

"Right, Jimmy," Levi said, checking for street signs, one directing the way to Twin Peaks, another declaring this was Market. Nothing looked familiar down here. What hadn't been smashed by the quake stood in the path of the inferno building at their backs.

"I'm Verna, and this is Agnes," Bird Cage said, taking long steps to keep pace. She said it was a pleasure to meet him, all of them, turning her head, telling Mabel she recalled seeing her at some church social or the like a month or so back, saying her and Agnes baked all them pies.

Mabel gave a weak smile.

"Well, this is no social," Levi said. "Best you save your breath for keeping up, ma'am."

Verna Culp stepped alongside Agnes Maier, keeping up with Levi, turning back to Mabel, taking Mack for the husband, saying to him, "Tall fellow's got a hard bark, don't see the harm in a little talk."

"Best do like he says, ma'am," Mack said, agreeing about the hard bark.

Smoke rolled over the rooftops, orange glowing behind the grey, the crackling from the Mission growing louder. Smaller fires popped up, showing at windows and doors. An upturned wagon lay in the street, a horse dead in its traces, killed by falling brick. The townsfolk moving around it. Buildings stood dark, the only light coming from the fires. Felt like they were walking through a dying city.

The ground gave a shiver, followed by a loud pop, flames whooshing from a ruptured gas main. Three Liquors, with several flats above, burst into flames, windows blowing out all at once. The people in the street scattered from it.

From an upper window, a man smashed out the remaining glass and leapt, several men running to him, carrying him to the opposite side of the street.

Leading the women past Sanchez, Levi pressed through the throng, Agnes and Verna right with him, bird cage and ironing board still in hand. Mack offering to take the baby a spell, Mabel saying she was fine, removing the frock, wrapping it around the baby.

. . . TRIAL BY FIRE

SOMEWHERE A siren wailed. Pressing along Market, Quinn figured to head up Stockton, guessing it would be less crowded. Wait for Levi Hayes, knowing the man would be lured by his own greed.

Fires bloomed at his back, his shirt and jacket wet with sweat. The people in the street packed tight, pressing for the waterfront, the whole godless city burning to the ground. Some looked resigned, some spooked like livestock in a storm.

Florence would be alone in that big house up on Nob Hill, her servants around her. As far as he could tell, there was no smoke over that part of town. He would deal with Hayes and Lewis, get the gold and the cockfight money, then go to her and tell how he set things right. Let the woman be grateful, hoping to pick up where they left off, Quinn remembering the feel of her, the smell of her hair. He hoped Levi Hayes had got killing Marvin right.

Stepping around a corpse skewered on an iron rod, pinned between sections of sidewalk, Quinn didn't give the man a second look, breaking from the crowd then, climbing a piano school's fire escape, stopping on the iron landing, seeing what lay ahead, the mass moving steadily, but slow. A billboard topping the hotel advertised Knox Hats.

A couple of men climbed into a storefront, where the front window had been, looked to be looting jewelry. A couple called up to him, pointing, wanting the copper to do something about it. Climbing down, Quinn advised he was on an errand of the highest order, suggesting if they wanted something done, they could go about it themselves, that or mind their own business and just keep moving. Turning from them, he had second thoughts on heading to Stockton, guessing Mission might be a better bet. From the glow and smoke over the rooftops, there were more fires in that direction, meaning fewer people in the street.

. . . OUTFLOWING

TRUDGING PAST Church and Fourteenth, then Dolores, the women showed exhaustion, the rubble in the street made the going slow. Hadn't made much more than a mile in the past hour, twice detoured by fire and wreckage blocking the streets. The air was hot and thick with smoke. Mounds of bricks lay scattered ahead, blocking a Peerless auto from going forward, water pooling around its wheels.

Splashing in the knee-deep water seeping and swirling from a fractured hydrant, turning the street into a river, Levi sloshed his way, grabbing the wheel of an overturned hansom cab. A chunk of brick cut into his bare sole, Verna catching his arm as he stumbled, forgiving him for his cursing.

Agnes slipped in the water, too, garments clinging to her skin. Reaching an arm, Mack helped her along, guiding Mabel with her baby, careful she didn't take a tumble, offering again to take the child. Mabel insisting she was alright.

They were moving too slow for Levi's liking. The heat

felt stronger at their backs. The roaring and crackling making it sound alive.

A man in a drooping sombrero led his daughter, calling the name of a lost loved one. Wading through the water, not heeding a merchant on horseback. The man coming at a gallop, saddle bags slapping the chestnut's flanks, the man's long coat flapping behind him. Slowing through the water, he yelled warning about the curtain of fire coming, wanting the crowd to clear a path. Knocking the man with the sombrero, the rider reined the horse, Mack towing Mabel out of its path. The rider clipped Verna, the woman reeling headlong, her hat knocked into the swirl.

Cursing, the rider slapped and urged his mount over a mound of bricks damming the street, his horse's hooves slipping, man and rider tumbling against the Peerless, the rider pitched into the stream.

Towing Verna to her feet, Agnes handed her the shapeless hat, Verna coughing, clutching her birdcage. The rider splashed before her, full of fight, the horse unable to rise. Spitting a mouthful of water, the rider yanked a pistol from his belt, aiming it wildly about, yelling for the horse to get up.

Jerking Agnes and Verna by their collars, Levi pulled them clear, the rider turning on the Peerless, shooting out a headlight, then aiming at the driver, the driver and passenger raising their hands. The crowd parted around the pool, the rider turning around and challenging any man.

Climbing past the windscreen and onto the hood, the driver dove at him from behind, knocking away the pistol, then throwing punches. The passenger, being an ample woman, struggled out her door, waded in and laid fists into the rider, punching like she was John L. Sullivan. Flanked, the rider fought back, swinging at one, then the other, before buckling under the blows. Other men waded in and tried to break it up, ended up throwing punches of their own. Most of the crowd kept moving.

Nudging Verna and Agnes through the water, Levi felt around, hoping to bump the rider's pistol with his foot. The suffering horse jerked to keep its head above the rising water, eyes wide with panic. Nothing anyone could do.

●

AT DOLORES and Market, two brothers grappled an upright Bechstein, the name on the piano's fallboard. Both with rolled shirtsleeves, they lifted it across the broken ground, getting as far the middle of the intersection. Setting it down, they mopped at their foreheads, muscles aching, looking at each other, knowing they'd gone as far as they could, the citizens passing on all sides. The brothers laid hands on the top, said some words, then left it and joined the movement for the waterfront. Leaving it to burn.

"Think Quinn had a hope?" Mack asked Levi.

"With the roof coming down?" Levi shrugged, shoving at a man cutting in front of him. The man turned and sized him up, saw Mack and thought better of starting anything. Keeping on his way.

"Think we used up whatever luck we had getting busted out," Mack said, looking at Mabel, realizing his mistake.

"Busted out?" She looked at him.

"Just a way of talking, ma'am."

"You men busted . . . saying you're convicts?" She stopped and drew back.

"More of a slight mix-up, ma'am," Levi said, looking at Mack.

"He said they got busted out." Mabel turned to Agnes and Verna, saying, "We're walking with convicts."

Taking her flask from a pocket, Verna uncapped it, saying to Mabel, "You got something they can steal?"

"Think our intent's plain, ma'am," Mack said. "At the Mission, not two days back. That drunk tugging on your arm . . ."

Her look said he was no different from the men along that wall.

"You ladies will do just fine on your own," Levi said, telling them to just keep moving for the ferry building.

"Come on, child," Agnes said to Mabel, dropping her ironing board, saying to Mack, "We do thank you, gents, and Verna and I will see them the rest of the way."

"They'll be fine," Levi said to Mack. "You forgetting we got business of our own?"

Mack looked at woman and child. Agnes and Verna helping her to the abandoned upright, middle of the street, water washing in from the broken main. The glow showing brighter over the rooftops from the south and east, smoke heaviest over the Mission. Windows that still had panes reflected the coming blaze. Air was getting hotter and harder to breathe. Ahead of them, the dome of the City Hall stuck up through the smoke, looked like it was sitting on a burned-out skeleton.

Half a block back, the motorist couple were back to beating on the rider, the woman holding him, her man punching away, the horse struggling to keep its head above rising water.

Another rumble, the ground shaking — this time from a dozen steers stampeding from the south. Faces turned and the crowd split, some jumping clear, one man knocked aside. Eyes wide and white with terror, the steers stampeded through, a young man swept under the hooves.

The motorists clambered for the hood of their auto, leaving the thrashing rider in the water. Agnes and Verna yanked Mabel and child up onto the upright.

A captain led his mismatched squad of Guardsmen in wake of the steers; one of the men stopped to put a bullet in the drowning horse, his corporal kneeling and firing his rifle up the street, into the steers.

Watching the craziness unfold, Mack left Levi standing there and dodged his way to the piano, grabbing Mabel down by the arm, saying, "You want to bury your child, that it?"

"Get your hands from me." She slapped and fought him.

Guardsmen ran by, ignoring them.

Nothing nice or gentle about it, Mack wrested the baby from her and sloshed through the water, Mabel hurrying in her slippers behind him, yelling for help, Mack telling her, "Be a hard-head all you want, but one way or another this child's going to safety."

She slapped and grabbed, but it was doing no good. The two women took hold of her, helped her past a longhorn lying in the street, a bloody hole in its throat. The crowd moved around it.

Levi waited on the steps of the church, its spire knocked out of plumb, the cross at the top gone. Cracks running through the word Adventvs chiseled into the stonework above the entrance. The quake had spared them from the rope, but out in the open, they were fine targets, Mack tempting fate, playing the hero with a child in his hands.

Soon as the Guardsmen had gone pursuing the steers, two men stepped from the wrecked Bank of California across the street, holding rifles and sacks, walking south, the opposite direction of the crowd.

Watching the world go crazy, Levi told the women, "You want to get to safety, then you keep close. That or you get left behind, that simple."

Between Agnes and Verna, Mabel stood and nodded, looking down at her ruined slippers, her feet hurting.

"Got no time for the stubbornness of women." If Quinn was alive, he'd get to the money first; it was that simple.

Agnes and Mabel looked at each other and shrugged.

"All right then," Levi said. He looked ahead of them, hadn't taken a step when he heard faint pounding from inside the church, a voice calling from behind the heavy door. Levi turning to Mack, his look saying, what the hell next?

Agnes Maier went and banged on the door, a voice calling from inside. Kicking away at the junk in front, she yanked on the handle but couldn't budge it. Verna joined, sweeping with her foot, trying to free the base of the door.

Cursing, Levi grabbed the end of a board, Mack passing the child to Mabel, catching hold of the other end.

The door was of thick oak; the quake had fractured the framework, jamming the door. Mack bucked his shoulder against it, Levi joining, the two of them doing it in tandem, the cracked frame giving way. A couple more tries and the door caved inward, Levi catching hold of the frame, Mack tumbling into the darkness, Agnes and Verna rushing in after him.

. . . CLOSING THE GAP

LOOKED LIKE froth seeping from the breached hydrant, wreckage floating in a whirling pool. Dipping his hat, Quinn drank without thinking about how dirty the water was, then tipped the hatful over his head. Shoving a fellow out of his path, he kept vigil, no time for the pain in his arm, holding the arm tight to his chest. Sharp-eyed, searching every face. His convicts were out here.

Out front of a store called the Emporium, four men rummaged like wild dogs through boxes of shoes scattered around the street. The blond one in a jacket of army blue was no more than eighteen. Full of drink, him and another man were holding bottles and shoes, one grabbing an armful of boxes, another trying on women's shoes, all of them laughing like fools, Enfields at their feet. The blond one stiffened at sight of the copper, tossing away a pair of lace-ups, bending for his rifle, clucking to the others.

Cocking his pistol, Quinn told him, "Touch it and you can forget about puberty."

Hands went wide in the air.

"Getting a jump on your holiday shopping, are you, boys?"

Holding his wine bottle, the blond one pointed to the Emporium's broken front window, saying, "Chased away a pack of looters, think it was my jacket that done it. Just putting all this back, Officer. Doing the same job as you."

All of them nodding, the one in women's footwear teetering.

"Looking for two men," Quinn said. "Grey-haired fellow, the other one younger, about my height. Both looking pretty beat up."

"That could be just about anybody," the one with the boxes said.

Belongings wrapped in a bed sheet, a heavyset man tripped into Quinn, sending a knifing pain. Quinn cuffed the man, knocking him to the ground, a rider on a bicycle swerving to avoid them, cursing Quinn, pedaling on.

The man on the ground squinted up, noting the number on Quinn's hat. Quinn pulling the pinned badge from his jacket, holding the seven-sided star in the man's face, letting him see the number real close, saying, "You got it?"

"Want no trouble," the heavy man said, getting to his feet, brushing himself off and moving on.

Holstering the pistol, Quinn stepped past the four men loading the shoes back through the broken window and pinned the badge back on.

... SAMARITANS

WEAK ON his legs, the reverend stepped through the door, blinked at the daylight, caked head to foot in plaster dust fine as flour, looking like the statue of a man chiseled from limestone. Dried blood lined the creases of his forehead, more dried blood in his hair. Looking up and down the street, then at the tilted spire above him, the old reverend disbelieved the destruction. About to speak when his legs gave out.

Catching him and easing him onto the fragment of a parapet, Levi looked for help. Lots of people in the street, but none of them stopping. One couple dragged an over-stuffed suitcase, the man on the bicycle shouting at them to clear the way.

Squatting and cupping the reverend's head, Agnes brushed the dust from his hair, seeing to his wounds saying, "Verna, your flask," snapping her fingers.

"Water would do him better," Verna said.

"You got any water?" Agnes asked, holding out her hand. Snapping. "The flask, Verna."

Looking at the flooded street, Verna pulled it from her skirt, handed it over, Agnes splashing whiskey on a fold of her skirt and dabbing at his gash.

Flinching at the sting, the reverend came awake and pushed the hand away. Caught the smell and took the flask from her and tipped a good swig; it set him coughing. Taking another swallow to ease the cough, he said, "Ah, God bless you, child."

"Easy there, Reverend, that's not milk." Verna reached the flask.

"Amen to that." His smile feeble, he let go of the flask.

Swishing the flask, Verna took a swallow herself, then tucked it away.

A couple, barely past their adolescence, pushed a baby buggy filled high with worldly goods. No baby, their faces hollow, their eyes vacant.

"Firestorm south of the Slot," one fireman called from the street, a rolled hose on his shoulder, hurrying against the flow of the crowd, saying to them the fire was racing up Tenth to beat the band, guessing they didn't have much time. Then he was heading for the worst of it.

Flames were higher now above the building tops, angry and dancing, the grey swirling above it. Levi helped the reverend to his feet, the man wobbling.

But his voice boomed: "Then the Lord rained upon Sodom and upon Gomorrah brimstone, and fire from the Lord out of heaven."

People looked from the street.

"Walking would do you better than preaching right now,

Reverend." Levi got the old man stepping, not liking the attention.

Being led along, looking to Verna Culp, the reverend said, "I'd say amen to another dram of that heavenly milk, child. Lends strength to the limbs."

Obliging, Verna asked his name as she watched him swig, more than half of it gone.

"Reverend Thadeus, ma'am. At your service." Recharged, he told Levi he could manage on his own now.

"Reverend, my Milton needs words said over him, if you're able." Mabel started to say how he met his end.

"Fire's not waiting on any last words," Levi said, pointing at the flames. "No offense, ma'am, but your man would surely want you and the baby to safety." Looking to Mack for help.

"That's so, ma'am," Mack said.

Assessing the flames, Thadeus said he'd keep it short, prayer knowing no distance or bounds. Being pointed in the direction of the fallen man, he took Mabel by the hand, Mack holding the child like she might break, having never held an infant. Levi scanning the crowd.

Smoke choked and stung their eyes, Mabel helped steady Thadeus, his words washing away sins and forgiving trespasses and temptations, ending with thine is the kingdom, and the power, and the glory.

"Right, then," Levi said, turning the old man to get them all moving, thinking he could be holding up the very reverend who'd be saying those same words over him and Mack if Quinn came along.

"You want, you go tend to business," Mack told Levi. "I'll see these folk to the Depot, then meet up later." The baby crying, tiny and pink, Mack bouncing her, his face grimy and unshaven, cooing and going, shh, shh.

A steam pumper was shoved past them, its five-man fire squad heading south to do battle. A banker dragged a laden trunk on a cart, his pistol tucked in his waistband, moving north with the crowd. Looking at the man, Levi judged his chances of wresting the weapon from him without getting shot.

●

MORE FLARE-UPS showed along Tenth, Levi getting the group as far as Market Square, the reverend barely on his feet. Flames in the upper windows of the Johnstone tower. A breeze was pushing in from the Bay, cool and holding the danger back, allowing rest for all those filling the Square.

The Victory Playhouse stood cracked open like an egg on the east side, its iron staircase spiraling at a strange angle, the roof crumbled, the upper floor exposed to the sky. A section of brick hung from an iron bar above the staircase, its fractured pillars rising to the roof beams. Bricks, plaster and shingles lay in mounds.

Perched on a marble step next to Mabel, Mack looked out at the milling folk, feeling his own weariness. Leaning against a pillar, Levi inspected his torn foot, looking back the way they had come, the spire of Reverend Thadeus's church gone from view now, smoke hugging at street-level. He couldn't see back as far as Van Ness.

The lodging house had been claimed, its sign declaring it the Fremont; a lumber store next door had caught fire and was belching smoke from its smashed-out windows. Smythe Bros. Wreckers stood next door; a billboard on the roof advertised building lots at Salada Beach for under three hundred bucks.

They had barely made more than a mile in the past hour. Mack getting all noble over the woman holding the baby. Levi not happy about it, pacing between busted pillars, leaving a bloody track in the ash and stone. If Quinn was alive, and if the Blazes was still standing, he'd beat them there and be waiting, wanting the gold, believing Levi and Mack had killed his brother.

Levi needed a gun.

Fixing Milton's frock around baby Emma, Mabel took her from Mack, the child all that was holding her together. Unfastening a button, she said to Mack, "I'll thank you to turn your head."

Flushing, understanding what she was doing, Mack said, "Gonna do that in the open?" Turning away.

"Rather she go hungry?" she said. First time Mabel smiled, allowing Emma to nurse. Mother, her little one — all there was in the moment.

Reverend Thadeus handed Verna the flask, with his compliments, saying, "Next one's on me." Confessing he was partial to gin and vermouth.

Shaking the empty flask, Verna said, "Gin and vermouth'll do fine." Smiling at this reverend imbibing the spirits. She started to toss the flask into the wrecked Playhouse, then stopped, realizing it was about the only possession she had left. She watched Levi go down the littered steps, pushing through the throng, heading for the opposite side of the Square. Worried he was leaving them.

Miller's Lodging House stood across and at an angle from the Playhouse. Most of its brick facade lay in the street, the interior exposed like a doll's house, half its framework in peril. A mother and her girls gathering their possessions in what had been their second-story flat.

More folks funneled in, the Square starting to look like a cattle drive. Bodies merged, some standing, some sitting, some trying to move along Market. Two boys pushed a bed tied atop a pair of bicycles, asking folks to make way. On top lay their invalid mother, calling over to the reverend, "We're blowing out of this town, right as rain, Reverend." Adding they wouldn't be at service Sunday.

Thadeus gave a wave, one of the boys saying it was too damn hard to eke a living with the good Lord causing such a thing.

"Wasn't by the hand of the good Lord, son," the reverend called back, thinking all these folks would be in need of church service come Sunday. And he would be there to give it, even if he had to stand in a field or on the end of a pier to do so.

Verna hadn't noticed it past all the heads till then. The Dubloon Saloon on the northwest corner was doing a rushing business, men going in, men coming out, resembling an ant colony. Drunken men thinking if they were doomed, they'd toast the devil and be in fine form. Looking at the flask, she told Agnes she'd be right back and went down the steps and swam into the stream of people, setting course for the saloon. Agnes calling after her, wondering if she'd plumb lost her mind.

Levi stepped into Miller & Franklin's Dry Goods, a single-story wood structure next door to the Dubloon. Otis Franklin clutched his double-barreled twelve-gauge, keeping vigil, nerves raw on account of the disorder next door: laughing and whooping men acting like it was any Saturday night.

Miller & Franklin's had survived the depression of the nineties, got past Franklin's wife dying of the influenza, and the earthquake shaking the whole city. Now it would face the fires, raging just a few blocks away, the Pacific breeze all that was holding it back. Otis Franklin hadn't seen a fire squad in the past hour.

Stepping on the plank step, Levi kept his hands wide, showing the man he was unarmed, asking if he was Miller or Franklin.

Leveling the barrel, not exactly aiming it, Otis said, "Either way, we're closed."

"See, the hubbub took my boots." Levi looked at his bare foot. "One of them, leastways."

"Suppose it got your billfold, too?"

"Didn't exactly allow for grabbing much of anything."

"And how do I know you're not one of these Barbary scum?" Otis nicked his head to the saloon, saying, "Drinking, likely to turn to looting."

"I look like I'm drinking or looting?"

Otis shrugged. "Look at these crazies."

Two juiced men do-see-doed, others clapping and stomping their feet, caroling the lyrics to "Sweet Rosie O'Grady."

"You come along, expecting me to just hand over footwear."

"That, and I could use a pistol."

Otis huffed.

"You know, mister," Levi said, "the fire finds this place, won't make much difference, will it?"

"Wind'll hold, and the fire brigade's on the way." Otis wagged the shotgun. "Now, get on with you, I got nothing for you."

"Best of luck to you, then," Levi said. Too tired to fight with assholes, he pushed his way back toward the Playhouse.

The baby was asleep, Mabel rocking and humming to her, Mack saying he'd be happy to hold Emma again for a while, let Mabel gain her strength. Looking at him, then letting him have the child, Mabel found humor in the way he held her, cradling Emma like she were the most unwieldy thing.

Coming up the steps, Levi looked doubtful at man and child, thinking this woman was working some mojo, having no problem with this jailbreaker now.

"Told you, go get on your way," Mack said, feeling his uncle's mood. "I'll meet up at the Depot or anyplace you say."

"Know you're sitting out in the open, right?" Levi said, looking into the Square, leaning against the column and yanking off his one boot, flinging it into the wreckage.

"Yeah, I know it, and my money says that son got flattened by the roof beam. So go on, go and get what's ours."

Mabel reached for Emma, telling Mack she wouldn't burden them any longer.

Swinging the baby from her reach, Mack said, "Don't you start up again. Nobody said nothing about you being a burden."

The baby began to fuss, Mack saying, "See what you done now," bouncing and cooing to her.

Levi turned to go, looking into the crowd again, a bad feeling staying with him.

. . . NARROWING THE GAP

PINNING THE body down with his foot, Quinn tore a strip from the dead rider's shirt, leaving the man floating in the pool before the abandoned auto. Holding a piece of dripping wood in place, he wrapped his forearm, enduring the pain and tugging it as tight as he could stand. His hand was swelling, the skin changing color. Nothing more to be done for it. Stepping around the dead horse, he kept moving.

Tilted power poles stood before a row of apartment houses, all in stages of ruin; the wood construction that had been no match for the quake now stood waiting to burn. As the crowd funneled past an abandoned carriage into the crowded Square, Quinn shouldered his way through, looking over the heads, making out the Dubloon on the west corner, the Victory Playhouse on the opposite side.

Then Quinn stopped, looking to be sure. Levi Hayes was wading through the bodies just ahead, only a half-dozen people between them. He watched him go up the Playhouse steps. Shoving a man aside, Quinn kept his eye on Hayes, the man he pushed cursing him in Spanish, wheeling Quinn by the arm, not hindered by the dirty uniform.

Facing him, Quinn drew and pressed his Colt into the man's belly. "Got some last words to say, amigo?"

Opening his hands, the man backed off, still muttering in Spanish as he went.

Taking off his hat, Quinn looked down and closed in, the Colt tucked inside the crown, cocked and ready.

Up on the Playhouse steps, Levi was pacing, talking to his nephew sitting on the steps next to a woman. The nephew was rocking an infant. Levi took a glance into the crowd, Quinn guessing he was watching for him. He didn't appear to be armed, and in a few more steps, Quinn would have them.

●

Leaving his dry goods to chance, Franklin stepped from his porch. What kind of God lets this happen? The wind was changing course now, the smoke starting to roll this way. At least the crowds would disperse, Franklin not so sure about the drunkards at the Dubloon, both his hands on the shotgun. Poured his life into that store, and by God, he'd protect it even if it was all doomed.

Slipping his way through the current of people, the shotgun tucked under an arm, Franklin got close to the Playhouse and called out, getting Levi's attention, "Reckon these'll fit."

Levi caught the moccasins.

"Best thing for your bleeding feet . . ." Franklin took twisted leather strips from a pocket and tossed them, too, saying, "Case they're a bit loose, shove those in the toes, give you a better fit."

Franklin didn't wait for a thank you, just turned and pressed his way back, bumping the gun barrel into a copper with a splinted arm, the man holding his hat out front. Yelping in pain, the copper turned away, Franklin saying he was sorry, telling him he ought to go do something about the goings-on at the Dubloon.

Levi didn't get a good look, but he knew it was Quinn ducking into the crowd, going around the carriage barring the way.

He didn't need the wadding, tossed the strips aside. Finding a fist-sized chunk of marble among the rubble, he left Mack to his cooing on the steps, and cut across the Square.

Wasn't how he'd seen facing Quinn, but he'd let it play out. Come up on the man and deliver a good crack across his skull. Duck past the Dubloon and be on his way. Catch up with Mack later.

•

JABBING A woman aside, Quinn squeezed past and angled for the Dubloon, the Colt inside the hat. Glancing back at the Playhouse, he lost sight of Levi Hayes, but he kept moving. Aiming to circle and double-back through the confusion and force the two into the alley, put the pistol to the nephew's head, force Hayes to tell where he hid the gold. Quinn stopped, hearing the shouts from past the Dubloon.

. . . THE DUBLOON

A SQUAD of soldiers moved double-time behind their sergeant and into the Square, coming from the north end.
Brandishing axes and shovels, rifles slung on shoulders. The
rabble parted or were shoved aside.

Half the squad hurried behind the square-jawed sergeant
into the Dubloon; the rest started rounding up men, drunk
or sober, plucking them from the commotion in the Square,
putting them into a line out in the front of the saloon. Some
voiced protests, a few raised fists. Someone hurled a stone,
and a soldier went down. Had the effect of a lit fuse. The
squad of soldiers charged into the drunks, smashing with
shovels and pick handles. Men sent to the ground, one with
a busted jaw, another flat on his face, bleeding from his nose
and mouth. A pistol shot rang out, and order was restored,
the soldiers going about reassembling the men.

A pickaxe was pressed into Levi's hands. Levi dropping
the chunk of brick, a hand shoving him forward. A soldier

with an ash-smeared face rousted him into the assembly, told him to shut his mouth and stand at attention. Levi glancing around for Quinn.

Shouts and the crash of chairs and bottles sounded from inside the Dubloon. On his porch, Franklin egged the soldiers on, offering the support of his buckshot.

Holstering his pistol, Quinn set the hat on his head, barking for those nearest to clear a path, told those closest they best heed the soldiers, pushing his way to the east side, aiming for the lane past the Playhouse.

A double stack of crates by a loading door allowed him to stay hidden and climb and peer out. Looking along the front of the Playhouse, seeing the nephew on the steps, still rocking the child. His eyes searched through the throng in the Square, catching sight of Levi being pressed into the ragged line out front of the Dubloon, a pickaxe in his hands. No way Quinn could get to him now.

Could end up as a damn stupid move, boasting about finding the money, telling Levi Hayes he left it in the cask, planning to deposit it after buying himself a verdict. Still, the man needed to die knowing that he'd been beaten on all fronts. And Quinn would get another chance. Somehow he was sure of that.

. . . PRESSGANG

Lieutenant Jinks sat on the big chestnut like he was on parade. The olive drab, the strapped leggings and blue cord made him infantry. The look of the man made him fresh out of the academy, an air about him like he lived by some spit-and-polish code. Reining in before the line of men, an army wagon clattering up behind.

Shouts and crashing lessened from the saloon. Staggering, bleeding drunks were shoved out the doors, the soldiers outside putting them roughly in line. One big private worked his way over to the Playhouse, motioning for Mack, coming up the steps, Mack giving him a boot down the steps. The soldier swinging the rifle from his shoulder, fight in his eyes. Mabel grabbed for the baby in Mack's arms.

"Not him," the lieutenant barked from across the Square.

The soldier looked at the officer, then re-slung his rifle, glaring at Mack like maybe they'd meet another time. Turning, he plucked the Spanish man by the scruff, forcing him over to the saloon, getting cursed in Spanish. Twenty men in the line, various stages of sobriety, a couple of soldiers holding rifles on them. Two men flat on the ground, one groaning, the other out cold, another dropping to his knees, hunching and retching.

Rough hands spun Verna Culp from the saloon, more hands cast her aside. Seeing Levi with a pick, she gave a slight wave, making her way past Franklin's, the man now sitting in his rocker, shotgun across his lap, enjoying the proceedings, watching the woman go, the flask in her hand, thinking her a harlot.

"I'm Lieutenant Jinks," the young officer called from his mount, his soldiers holding the line. "And this establishment is hereby closed."

Shouts of dissent from the line of men, the barkeep ramming his way through the saloon doors, holding a whiskey bottle in the air, defying the officer, calling him baby-face, his voice booming across the Square, "And I say, it's a free country, and the next one's on the house, boys." Waving everybody back in.

The cheer that rose was halfhearted, a couple of the men starting for the door, the lieutenant drawing his sidearm, his horse rearing as he fired in the air.

"It ain't right," the barkeep protested, the wind's change of direction giving him maybe an hour to rake in what he could before the place went up in flames. "You got no fucking right interfering with a citizen making his last bit of livelihood. Ain't things bad enough? Now come on, boys."

Extending his arm, Jinks shot the bottle from the barkeep's hand, the bullet buried in one of the *o*'s in the word *Dubloon*, the wooden sign swinging next to the door. Raising the pistol and putting it on the barkeep, Jinks said, "At least it's living, sir." Then to the crowd, "By order of General

Funston and this pistol, any man-jack not complying with said orders will find himself dispatched right here in the street. Sergeant Booth, post a man by that door. Anyone tries to enter, shoot the bartender."

"Yes, sir." The sergeant stepped up next to the barkeep, looking happy to oblige, drawing the Colt from its holster, crossing his arms, waiting for any man to try.

Throwing the bottle neck down on the steps, the bartender said, "Fine, I'm fucking closed," wishing an untimely and fiery end to the lieutenant, spitting at the sergeant's feet, shouldering back through his doors, kicking over a chair.

"Hear me now," the lieutenant called out. "Rooming house called the Portland's collapsed with women and children trapped inside. You gentlemen volunteering are lending a hand to get them out. Now, let's not misspend another minute. Lives are at stake." Turning his mount.

Some of the men sobered, one yelled it was the army's business, somebody asking if the lieutenant knew the fucking meaning of volunteering. The lieutenant told his men to feel free to deal with the next one that opened his mouth any way they saw fit. Rifles were unslung and bolts were thrown. Silence followed.

The balance of the men were outfitted, soldiers going to the back of the wagon, shoving spades and shovels into their hands. A forced march like a chain gang. Jinks angled his mount through the refugees, within calling distance of Mack, thinking him a family man, next to his wife and child. "Head right up Market, sir, get yourselves to the ferry building. Got soldiers there to take care of you." Looking at Thadeus, he said, "If you're able, preacher, there'll likely be prayers in need of saying."

The old man nodded, Agnes helping him to his feet.

·

QUINN WATCHED from behind the crates, the line of men led from the Square. A soldier at arms out front of the saloon, meaning Quinn couldn't get at the nephew.

Smoke rolled into the lane, thick and choking, the heat coming behind it. His best bet was to make his way along Fourth or Third, then head up Stockton or Grant, whichever was clear, and get to the shipyards. Take his money from the cask and wait.

·

THE STENCH of burning rubber rose from the Akron factory, ash drifting into the Square like snow. It was time to move. Passing Emma to Mabel, Mack got the women to their feet, told them to keep step, lending Mabel a hand down the steps, going past the mouth of the alley lined with crates, the crowd starting to move from the Square.

. . . PORTLAND HOUSE

Lieutenant Jinks led his ragtag column double-time up Market and over to Mission. The bellyaching stopped, volunteers keeping step with the soldiers. His horse blew, nostrils quivering, sensing what lay ahead, not liking the chosen path, Jinks patting its neck. The Portland House stood on Sixth. Scanning the mess of the street, Jinks judged the west side passable enough. Speaking easy to his horse, he urged it on.

The private driving the wagon steered around a flipped railcar, putting two wheels up on the walk. Marching at the rear of the mix of volunteers and soldiers, the pick across his shoulder, Levi watched for his chance, the ash-faced soldier the last man behind him.

Reverend Thadeus sat in the bed of the wagon, his feet dangling off the back, the wheels bumping over the rubble. Offering up a prayer for a man ushering his family, hastening them in the opposite direction.

The father called to the soldiers, letting them know the Royal had caved in at Fourth, same as most of the other lodging houses around it. Putting his arm around his wife, he guided his daughters along.

... KILL EDICT

THE DOOR opened, and two men exited Folsom Clothing, stepping into the strange grey of mid-morning, each juggling a tower of garments, men's suits and ladies' dresses, their chins steadying the stacks. First man out was gangly, called himself Tipsy, followed by Elmer Epps, Marvin Healey's carpenter, a slouch hat pulled low, a bandage across his nose.

"Well, look at that booty," Quinn said, leaning against the porch rail, retying the cloth around the splint. He had lost sight of the nephew a block back, stopped to rewrap the wrist, watching these two through the window.

Tipsy jerked back, nearly dropping his stack. His Navy Colt tucked in his belt, he considered his play, knowing Quinn by reputation. He looked up the street, but the rest of the group had gone on, searching for plunder.

Quinn grinned, recognizing Elmer as Marvin's head carpenter, saying, "It's a small world."

Elmer agreeing it was, set to drop the armload, guessing they had a chance to clear their pistols. Be more than happy to kill this Healey, even the score for what the brother had done to him at Pearly's.

Quinn nodded at the man hurrying his wife and girls along, the same family that had passed Jinks and his men on the way to the Portland House, the man not wanting anything to do with a lawman dealing with the lawless.

"It's all going to burn, Officer Quinn," Elmer said, balancing the stack with one arm, looking at the family hurrying away.

"Could see it as us getting these things to safety," Tipsy said.

"Guess I could." Quinn grinned.

"Not much good to anybody all burned up, and adding to the fires," Tipsy said. Ready to make his own play, he shifted the stack to one hand, freeing the other.

The pistol came up, Quinn cocking it in one motion, the barrel in Tipsy's face. "What you got under there? Sidearm?"

"Well . . . think so . . . not so sure it's even loaded."

"Not much good that way."

Tipsy shifted the stack of clothes, taking it in both hands, glancing at Elmer.

"Either of you boys read?"

"Yu . . . yeah . . . some," Tipsy said.

"How about you?" Quinn said, shifting his aim to the carpenter. "Elmer, isn't it?"

"That's right, Officer Quinn," Elmer said, happy the man recognized him, thinking it could help. "Elmer Epps, your good brother's chief carpenter. Have been now for —"

"Asked if you can read?" Quinn nodded to a posting on the porch beam.

"This here situation ain't what it seems, per se," Tipsy said, stepping close, trying to block the copper, give Elmer a chance to pull and shoot.

"Read." Quinn gestured to the notice, newly tacked on the beam out front of the store, the same notice the army was busy tacking on posts across town.

Stepping close, Tipsy squinted. "Proc . . . procla . . . ahh, shit . . . didn't bring along my specs."

Quinn stepped closer, touching the pistol to Tipsy's side, keeping Elmer in sight, reading, "'Proclamation by the Mayor' . . . says, 'the federal troops, the members of the regular police, and all special police officers have been authorized to kill any and all persons found engaged in looting or the commission of any other crime.'" Quinn looked at Tipsy, then Elmer. "You with me?"

Both men nodding.

"But that just ain't right," Tipsy said, "I voted for E.E. Schmitz. Met him once whilst he was pressing the flesh. But, if you say so, we'll just put these things back if you think it best. Won't be no harm —"

Elmer picked then to draw, and Quinn shifted and shot him through the stack. Staggering back, Elmer dropped the clothes, trying to stay on his feet. Felt like the wind got punched out of him by a giant fist, his knees going weak. Looking down and touching the spreading wet on his shirtfront, he couldn't believe he'd been shot.

Flinging his pile of clothes, Tipsy dove against the wall as Quinn fired again. Missing.

Clearing his Colt, banging into the wall, Tipsy got off a wild shot, then a second.

Diving off the porch and firing back, Quinn rolled over his broken wrist. Screaming.

"How you like it, som'bitch?" Tipsy yelled, feet planted wide, shooting too high, thinking he'd hit Quinn.

Quinn rolled in the dirt, both men snapping off shots, Tipsy backing against the wall, firing down, and Quinn on his back, firing up. Both missing again. Jumping behind the post, Tipsy fired his last round, Elmer bleeding at his feet. The click told him he was empty, Quinn's bullet boring through the proclamation.

"Stay put, Elmer, I'm going for help." Throwing the pistol at Quinn, Tipsy leaped through the doorway, hoping for a back way out, the others likely over on the next street. "We'll be back for you, Elmer. Deal with the som'bitch."

Quinn fired through the window, glass exploding, Tipsy dropping behind the counter. Quinn couldn't tell if he hit him, but the man didn't come back up.

Getting up on one knee, Quinn looked around the quiet street, heard the distant flames crackling and roaring. Wedging the pistol into his elbow, he reloaded, getting to his feet and stepping back up on the porch. Eyes searching inside Folsom Clothing, Quinn nudged Elmer with his boot, glass crunching underfoot. "Still with us, Elmer?"

Catching the moan, Quinn knelt and frisked the man's pockets, keeping an eye on the storefront, taking the cash Elmer had pilfered from the till. The ring on his finger looked made of gold. "You know Levi Hayes and his nephew?"

Shaking his head, Elmer balled his fingers into a fist, trying to hide the ring, wincing from the pain, Quinn uncoiling the fingers. Elmer saying it belonged to his mother. "All I got of her."

"More likely stolen." Quinn saying, "'Fraid I got to take

it into evidence. Course, if it's true, then the good news is you and Mother about to be reunited." Pressing his foot down on Elmer's wrist, Quinn tugged on the ring.

Elmer screamed, unable to pull away.

"About Hayes's nephew . . . you seen him . . . with a woman?"

Elmer just shook his head.

Drawing his boot knife, Quinn let Elmer have a look, saying, "You sure?"

Elmer shook his head again, wild eyes on the blade.

"Be a help if you'd hold still." Quinn clamped down and pressed the blade into the hand.

Elmer screamed, yanking and shrieking for Tipsy.

"Sure the nephew didn't come this way?" Looking in the store, Quinn pressed, drawing some blood.

"Both of them . . . just before . . . run right by." Elmer nicked his head up the street, his eyes going back to the knife. "That way, Hayes and Lewis, both of them, running like hell."

Quinn sliced through the fingers, easy as cutting carrots.

Elmer howled, tugging like mad, blood spurting from the stumps.

Cracking the pistol butt into his jaw, Quinn silenced him, twisting the ring free of the mangled stump. Pocketing it, he swiped away the finger bits, then plunged the knife hilt deep into Elmer's chest.

Looking up the street, Quinn pulled the blade free and wiped it on a dry spot on Elmer's shirt, then wiped his hand, the blood spreading from both wounds. Sliding the knife into the sheath inside his boot, he watched Elmer die. Must have hit the lung, the way the air came out of the man, groan coming from the mouth. Getting up, Quinn glanced inside the broken storefront for the other one, either gone or dead. Didn't matter.

Then he kept moving.

. . . SQUARED AWAY

TACKING THE mayor's proclamation on a pole with the butt of his Colt, the militia man stood not two blocks from Folsom Clothing, sure he heard pistol shots over the howl of the fire.

"'I have directed all the gas and electric lighting companies not to turn on gas or electricity until I order them to do so,'" Mabel stood reading. "'You may therefore expect the city to remain in darkness for an indefinite time. I request all citizens to remain at home until order is restored. Signed, E.E. Schmitz, the Mayor.'"

"What home would that be?" Agnes Maier asked the man.

"If your home's gone, ma'am," the militia man said, "then best keep heading for the docks. Ferries and anything floating will take you folks to Alameda and Oakland. Hear the army's springing camps up. Got earthquake shacks at Golden Gate, more going up at the Presidio. All with food and water and medical supplies coming in. All under control."

"Under control?"

"Doing the best we can, ma'am." He finished tacking the notice. "You get yourselves over there, you'll get squared away." He took his stack of notices, moving up the street.

. . . DELIVERANCE

The Portland House had sunk into the ground, tilted like it was in a quagmire, the third-floor windows barely above ground level, the lower floors crushed. The building reduced to a squeezebox, any inhabitants still alive inside were trapped in apartment tombs. An outfit of reserve firefighters were on the scene, totally worn out, covered in sweat and soot, having pulled those they could to safety, the wounded sitting in the street, the dead lined along the far curb.

Soldiers and volunteer rescuers set to work, aiding the wounded who couldn't walk on their own, getting them to the wagon. Reverend Thadeus stood in the bed, helping where he could, lifting them with prayer.

Working alongside the men climbing into the mess, Levi got to the building and cleared away a timber, scraping away rubble with the pick, listening for cries, looking for anyone trapped below. An eye on the advancing wall of fire. His body covered in sweat from the incredible heat.

The ash-faced soldier who had grabbed him back in the Square toiled beside him, saying his name was Darby, handing Levi a pair of boots he took off the back of the wagon, saying, "Be a better bet for scrambling over this shit." Not saying who they had belonged to.

Levi nodded thanks, forcing his feet in and stuffing the moccasins into his back pockets. The two of them set to clearing a section of crumbled stone from around a half-buried archway.

"Served with the squad at the Brunswick Hotel at Sixth and Howard at first light," Darby said, clearing boards, saying how the building had crumbled to the ground with all three hundred rooms occupied. "Hundreds feared alive under the tumbled walls. Damned fires sweeping through with such a force." He shook his head, tears in his eyes. "Nothing for us to do but leave them and run. Tell you, I live to be a hundred, I won't stop hearing them cries over the roar of flames. All them doomed and us running."

"No sense dying, too." Levi turned, looking back at the wall of fire blasting heat and pushing this way. Partially sheltered by the back of the Portland House, he knew they'd be pushed back soon.

Darby kept clearing boards, saying of his squad one was a cousin, another a grade-school chum, both perished under falling timbers.

Working away at the wreckage, Levi chopped away at stonework with the pick, prying up boards that Darby cleared, both of them looking through slots and gaps into the crushed floors.

The white of a garment caught his eye, Levi calling, "Darby, here!"

Levi swung the pick, making a space, a glimpse of a

figure lying among the broken slats inside the sunken floor. Darby dug away until the gap was wide enough to crawl into. "I'll go." Not waiting to discuss it, Levi slid down.

The man was unconscious but alive, his one arm looked crushed. A wet wheezing sound when he breathed. Freeing the arm, Levi eased the man onto a section of door, searching the tight space for anyone else before pushing the door up to Darby like a stretcher, steadying the injured man by the boot-heels, keeping him from sliding off.

"I got him," Darby said, pulling the man up.

Crawling up after, Levi pushed his end of the door until they had the man out.

While they carried him on the busted door, the man's arms and legs flopped down. They made it to the now crowded wagon, the reverend helping to ease the man down, the white of the man's radius bone poking through the pulped skin.

More dead had been lined along the curbside. Men, women and children.

Wiping his brow under the campaign hat, Jinks called a corporal to him, ordering him to search out a plot of ground suitable for shallow graves. Hoping they had time to temporarily bury the dead. Keeping an eye on what was coming, Jinks knew time was running out, his horse stamping the ground, nostrils flaring and eyes wild.

The wounded unable to walk were packed up onto the crowded wagon, some on the laps of others. Those who could walk milled around the wagon and held fast where they could, some propping others up.

Darby and Levi and a half-dozen others made a final sweep around the far side of the Portland House, the men scrambling over a bank of brick and boards. The ground at the rear was starting to smoke like a peat bog, the men unable to cross it now, the howl of the fire growing louder, coming closer, blocking out any last cries for help. The incredible heat pushing them back on the double. Climbing atop a tumbled wall, Darby peered down into a window half-covered by earth and debris. The ground giving way and the wall caving in, Darby plunging into the smashed basement. Throwing himself down, Levi crawled to the hole, looking down after the man, calling his name.

"I'm alright." Coughing, Darby got his legs under him, looked like he'd fallen into what had been an apartment. In the half-light streaming through the broken walls, he found a woman, her legs pinned under a bed, a dresser tipped on her. The woman was dead, but he wasn't leaving her. Shoving the dresser aside, he lifted her, hoisting her up to Levi. Catching her under the arms, Levi pulled the body through the opening, easing her to the ground.

Extending his arm down the hole, he tugged Darby out, Darby slinging the woman to his shoulder, Levi keeping Darby steady, the two of them taking her out front to the curb, laying her in line. Both looking down at the woman until Jinks called them away.

Couldn't get near enough for a handhold on the wagon, Levi stood at the rear, the men assembling, the heat like a fire pit. Thinking of Pearly for the first time since the quake struck, seeing her safe up in her boudoir, drinking her fine whiskey and playing that Nellie Melba on her Victrola. Word from Jinks was that the Western Addition had been spared so far. Meaning Pearly's and the House of Blazes might have gone unscathed.

. . . PARIS OF THE PACIFIC

STILL MORNING and it was evening dark, a livery burning and sending up black smoke, the air hot and holding little oxygen. Mack's clothes stuck to his skin and reeked of smoke. Cradling the crying infant, he walked ahead of the women, leading them.

Few words between them now, the women were exhausted, Mabel doing her best to keep step, in her nightdress, feet hurting inside the slippers, a hand on Mack's arm, touching a damp kerchief to Emma's mouth, wiping at her sweet face, the baby coughing and crying between bouts of fitful sleep.

The crowds had thinned; the street had been destroyed. Walking around a rupture several hundred feet long, about a foot wide, there was no telling how deep it was. Trolley rails had been torn up in the street, twisted like ribbon. A post office door hung from a single hinge, a pair of workers inside beating at flames with mail sacks. Boxes of post had been carried out and dumped into the street.

A pumper squad fought a blaze inside a four-story insurance building beyond hope. A fireman, looking like he'd applied blackface with white around his eyes, called to them, "Can't get through ahead." He waved his flat cap, trying to get them off Market, calling, "O'Farrell's your best bet," said something more, his words becoming lost in the roar.

Ruptured mains were making the fire squad's battle impossible, but, to a man, they were giving it a brave front. The street around them had turned to another river of useless water. Steam was hissing around the foundation, a couple of the men pulling their pumper back to the middle of the street, spraying what water they had left through the shattered second-story windows, the insurance company's interior mostly devoured.

A terrific roar followed a blast of flame from the upper windows, a couple of the firemen hurled to the ground, the hose twisting like a reptile, wild and spraying in the street.

The roof collapsed inward, the front wall arcing out and crumbling into the street, one of the men buried. The others rushed to him, none retreating.

"Wait here," Mack said to the women, passing Emma to her mother. "Get under that doorway." Mack pointed to the nearest building, then hurried across the intersection, going to help.

The fireman in the street waved the displaced away, looked at Mack coming, turned with him and went to help his crew. "Whole town's going to hell." Pointing to the top of the Call Building showing above its skeleton in the distance. "You believe it?" Billows swirled around its baroque dome and copulas. "City Hall and the Hall of Records both burning beyond it." The two of them hurried to the buried pumper, helping the injured men back as more of the building tumbled down.

Embers floated across from the insurance building, Mabel swatting at them, shielding Emma in her arms, Agnes and Verna on either side of her, doing the same, the three standing inside the curved archway, all eyes on Mack, waiting on his return. Some of the people who had been watching from the street moved past them, seeking a new detour to the ferry building.

Relieved when she saw him coming back, Mabel let Mack take the child, brushing some of the black from his jacket, walking along with him, Mack saying they'd try to cut over to Larkin. "Have to detour past Geary, get ahead of the fire." Not saying he was moving them farther from the Depot to do so.

The crowds were gone and people were few as they crossed what he guessed was Sutter, no street signs to give him a bearing, buildings on all four corners smashed and tumbled down, the rooftops gone, rafters and struts sticking through. Best guess, they were only blocks from Stockton. Nothing looking right to him, this San Francisco created in some vision of hell.

A few stragglers turned up ahead, heading back to Leavenworth, saying they didn't like the look of the smoke up ahead.

Still their best bet, Mack figured, to cut along Mason, the fires rerouting them to Jackson. Getting them nearer to Pearly's than to the ferry building, Mack thinking they could stop there, maybe get some water, take Pearly with them — if she hadn't gone already.

The women followed, none questioning him. A mongrel wandered from the rubble, coming to him, sniffing and eyeing the women, then moving off the way the stragglers had gone.

Halfway up the block, Mack stopped. Three drab men came from an alley, turning their way, fanning across the road, checking in doorways and windows, each carrying packs, rifles over their shoulders. Not regular army or militia. Having seen enough grubbers in his time, Mack turned the women around.

"Looks clear enough," Mabel said.

"Trust me," he said, leading the way back to the intersection, looking past his shoulder, his eye on the men.

"Those men . . ." Mabel remembering the proclamation.

He nodded and headed west another block, the street abandoned, buildings on either side showing heavy damage, most of the windows smashed out. Mack gave another glance back, kept on walking.

Mendelsohn's Feed had lost half its clapboard, boards piled across the porch and entrance. A wagon on its side looked like someone had tried to barricade the street, the front axle snapped, the bed smashed in, grain sacks dumped on the ground. A mule lay dead in its traces, skin along its flank ripped wide, its mouth pulled back, teeth frozen in a lifeless smile.

Scrambling atop a pile of clapboard, Mack lent a hand to the women, one at a time, helping them over, telling them to watch for nails. Then told them to hold up while he poked around the sundry next to Mendelsohn's. Clearing junk from in front of the door, he went in, the structure looking about to collapse, its walls at strange angles, boards and beams ripped and cracked. The roof slumped to one side. The interior was dark; Mack found nothing of use.

A few doors up, the Roll o' Dice Dry Goods looked in

better stead, in spite of a sloping porch roof. He tried the door. Locked or jammed. Picking up a length of board, Mack told the women, "Turn away."

Mabel started to object, Mack spiking the board through the glass. He punched it out, knocking away the shards from the frame.

"What in God's name . . ." Mabel said, stepping away.

"Wait there," he said, stepping through, not sticking around for questions.

Standing where he left them, Mabel looked to Agnes and Verna, the three of them drawing close.

"'Trust me,' he says," Mabel said.

"Got a better idea?" Agnes said, brushing a shoe at the shards of glass. First to settle on the walkway, her limbs throbbing, she repeated his words, "The man knows what he's doing. May as well sit, let him do it."

Verna sat, then Mabel, rubbing her hand across Emma's back, adjusting Milton's frock. Rocking the fussing baby, Mabel hummed to her, her mouth close to the baby's ear, afraid Emma's crying might attract the attention of the men they had seen just a few streets back. The type of men from out front of the Mission, that day she first saw Mack Lewis.

Rocking Emma, she allowed her thoughts to drift to Milton for the first time since the reverend had said his words in the street. Tears coursed her cheeks, thinking of him lying out front of their home like that. Nothing she could do to help him. Not daring to imagine what had become of him since. Any man deserved better.

Brushing her hand through Emma's fine hair, she hugged her close and kissed her forehead, hearing Mack rummaging inside.

"Let me take her a minute," Verna said.

Shaking her head, meaning she was okay, Mabel smiled through her tears, picturing what Milton would say if he could see her sitting here, waiting on a jailbreaker to loot a store before taking her and Emma on to safety.

"What's funny?" Verna asked.

"Here we all are . . ." was all Mabel said.

Taking the flask the bartender had filled at the Dubloon before the soldiers marched on the Square, Verna offered first sip to Mabel, hearing Mack crashing around inside. "Wet your throat?"

Mabel hesitated, then took it and sipped, coughing, guessing what Milton would have had to say about that, too. A nursing mother imbibing in the street.

"Just busted out of jail," Agnes said, nicking her head at the shop. "Suppose he can't help himself."

Now Mabel was laughing, the others joining in.

"Guessing sight of the other looters set him off," Verna said.

More laughing, the whiskey passed around, all three dismissing notions of Mack ducking out a back door, leaving them on their own.

"What the hell's he after, anyway?" Agnes took the flask, letting some more burn down her throat, then passing it to Verna.

"He said wait," Mabel said, "and that's all there is to do." She was first to see the man coming, rifle in his hands. She pushed herself to her feet.

•

THE PLACE looked ransacked, overturned shelves, emptied baskets, drawers left hanging. No cash in the till. Mack rummaged a stack of Strauss's trousers, bottles of preserves smashed and pooled around his feet, the clothing sopping up the juice. Finding a pair that weren't stained, he judged the size and guessed they might be close, shaking dust from them. Found a flannel shirt and a pair of shoes by an over-turned rack, measuring the size by spanning his hand, front to back. Guessing they'd have to do.

Stepping back through the smashed window, he said, "Afraid these are the best I cou—"

The two spinsters sat petrified, their eyes on the soldier sighting down his carbine.

Buttoning her nightdress, Mabel passed Emma to Verna, got up, shielding Mack.

"Sit back down, lady. I got my orders," the soldier said, trying to sight past her. Barely past his first shave, he looked from one to the other, wondering what the hell to do. Couldn't just shoot the man with the women and a baby looking on.

"And what might they be, pray tell?" Mabel asked him, hands at her hips, blocking any shot.

"We've been authorized to . . . deal with persons found engaged in the act of looting," the soldier said like he was reading it off the proclamation. "So if you got any last words to say, best say them."

"A man providing in a time of need is hardly engaged in any such thing."

"Told you to sit down, lady," the soldier said, trying to hold on to his authority, jabbing the air with the carbine's barrel, repeating, "I got my orders."

"And such orders are best carried out with a modicum of thought," Verna said, passing the baby to Agnes, getting up next to Mabel, putting a hand over the man's gunsight, pushing the barrel aside.

"Hey!" The soldier pulled it back, taking a step back, trying to point it at Mack.

"This man was appointed by your very own Lieutenant Jinks to take us to safety," Verna said, pointing behind her to Mack. "Suppose you've heard the name?"

The soldier flinched. The two women blocked any shot, another one sitting with an infant. All this craziness. He'd just come from Portsmouth Square, the police chief ordering the rescue of records from the doomed Hall of Justice, officers with him pouring bottles of beer from the tavern across the street, soaking the canvas bags, saving records with suds. One of the men unbuttoning his trousers, urinating on the papers.

"Why, you're no more than a boy." Passing the baby to Mack, Agnes stepped up, too, saying, "You can't want bloodshed on your hands, boy." She turned to Agnes. "Imagine him leaving Mabel a widow and Emma just an orphan."

"Carrying that with him all his days," Agnes said. "Never to have a proper night's sleep ever again."

"Can't hardly think what the good lieutenant would have to say about it," Verna said.

"Likely execute him, boy or not."

The soldier backed another step.

"And that man's got a rapid boil to be sure," Agnes said to Verna. "Got the reputation for asking questions once he's calmed himself, so I hear."

"I stand here in my nightdress, sir," Mabel said, looking down at her dirty feet, standing with Agnes and Verna. "I'm hardly decent, and you deny me proper attire."

"No, I . . ." The soldier tipped the rifle up, giving up, asking how they'd come to know Lieutenant Jinks anyhow. The only thing he was sure of, he wasn't shooting anybody.

Not this day. Likely be lucky to get away unscathed from these hens.

"Just spoke to him scarcely an hour ago," Mabel said.

"Right over on Market," Agnes said. "In all his glory on that chestnut mare. Right where he told this good man to escort us to safety. Best way he knows how."

"Alright. Well, I guess it's a special case, then." He relaxed hold on the carbine, looking at the smoke swirling only blocks away. "Ask me, I'd say your best bet's Broadway." He looked past the women to Mack, saying to him, "Take you straight to the water."

"Obliged," Mack said.

"And we thank you for that," Mabel said, and turned to Mack, taking the clothing from him, telling him to hold on to his darling Emma while she got herself decent. Smiling, she enjoyed the moment, turning back to the soldier boy. She started to unbutton the top of her nightdress.

Slack-jawed, the soldier shuffled his feet, forced his gaze away, not sure where to put it, standing the rifle butt in the dirt.

"If you're going to double our escort, we'd be grateful," Mabel said, "but I expect you've got soldiering to tend to." Buttons unfastened, letting Emma have the breast.

"Yes, ma'am," he said, tipping his cap, careful to keep his eyes turned down the street, happy to head off in that direction.

"Saw a couple of fellows prowling just a while back," Mack said to him. "Couple of streets over." He pointed away from the looters they had seen.

The soldier boy nodded and headed toward Van Ness, happy to get away.

. . . LAW DOG

BOOTS CLANKED up the fire escape. The Sentinel Hall Building was nothing but a steel skeleton, Quinn looking across another temporary morgue from the second-story landing. Militia and firemen taking carted bodies from wagons and autos. Some shallow graves had been dug and stakes pounded to mark the temporary sites, but not enough of them. And no way of identifying most of the dead. The men filled the graves, then lined the rest of the bodies in the street.

Climbing back down, Quinn moved away, keeping from sight of the militia. Busted pipes jutted from a disemboweled branch of the First National, its doors lying in the entry. A body lay face down, bottom of the steps, center of the street, arms and legs splayed, the shoes gone, the flesh so cooked it looked like it might fall away to the touch. No telling if it was a man or woman.

Ahead, Quinn watched as tendrils of smoke crept low along the street, thick and grey. The diversion around the

Square had cost him time, and he'd lost both Levi and the nephew. But, Quinn was sure, he'd get another chance.

And Florence would be his, too, Marvin offed by the very low-gamers Quinn would kill. Maybe get it done today. Avenging his brother would likely elevate him to toast of the town — what was left of it, anyway. Filling Marvin's shoes and sitting at his desk, sleeping in his bed and having his woman.

The stone walls of the First Union stood windowless, the roof and beams gone. Another sewer main had ruptured, more useless water pooling on the cobblestones. Cabinets and furniture had been tipped into the street, papers floated or danced in the air. Quinn walking by it all, didn't matter at all.

A pair of policemen pushed through the door, carrying metal boxes. Flynn and Boyers, both by-the-book assholes from the Hall of Justice over at Kearney. Two men Quinn had under him, the two he'd called on years back to raid the House of Blazes. That crazy bouncer Nikko sapping Quinn, taking all their guns, then their uniforms and badges, and kicking them into the street.

"Well, well," Flynn said, recognizing him, glancing at Boyers, both men smiling.

A city official in bowler and waistcoat followed behind, calling for Quinn to come lend a hand.

Showing his makeshift splint, Quinn called back, "Would, but I'm on special assignment, and time's of the essence."

Flynn and Boyers looked at each other, the official saying, "On whose orders?"

"No time for this," Quinn said, and kept walking.

"Afraid I must insist. These documents . . ." The official looked to the two officers, saying, "Do something."

Holding the metal case, Flynn said, "Where you want them?"

Quinn walked on to Montgomery Square — not getting pressed into the service of saving a city that was lost. He cut down a side street that looked like it had taken cannon fire, mortar and brick lying in chunks, boards sticking up. Looking back to see that Flynn and Boyers weren't following, he picked his way over the wall of a fallen bark shed, heedful of snags and gaps, practically sliding down the other side.

Halfway along the side street, Quinn stumbled on a grey-haired man, near-hidden under some brick and board at the rear of a tannery. The man's skin was drained of color, his legs pinned under a beam, bone sticking through. The man's eyes opened, looking up at Quinn. "Thank God."

Swiping a foot at the debris around the man, Quinn looked back for Flynn and Boyers, assessing. "Don't thank Him yet, friend."

"How's it look?" The man glanced at his legs.

Flames showed from the four-story at the lane that split in either direction, about two hundred feet away, fire feeding on what lay in its path.

"Be honest with you, friend, I wouldn't exactly go calling you lucky." Quinn bent and put his back into it, trying to budge the beam. Not a chance with only one good arm.

"Can't feel them — my legs. They look busted?"

"One for sure," Quinn said, looking at the odd angle of the leg, the bone sticking through the pant leg. "Hard to say how bad." Bucking his back into it, Quinn tried again. Even if he got the old man loose, he sure wasn't going to walk out of here, and no way Quinn could carry him through this choking air with only one good arm. Could go back for Flynn and Boyers.

Licking cracked lips, the old man glanced in the direction Quinn was looking, then back, seeing the fire spreading to a neighboring rooftop, coming this way, knowing what it meant, feeling the panic.

"What's your name?" Quinn asked.

"Howard Sommers."

"Well, Howard, best I can do is go for help. Couple of my boys on the next street. How's that sound?"

"Sounds damned good." Howard Sommers looking up at him.

Reaching a hand, Quinn felt inside Howard's vest, took out his billfold.

"What the hell you doing?"

Wagging the man's billfold, Quinn said, "The kind of help I'm talking about's going to need some swaying."

"Your boys, you said. Mean police?"

"All got a price this day." Pocketed the bills, tucked the empty billfold back in Howard's vest. He wasn't going back for Flynn or Boyers, those two not the type to stick their necks out; still, he wanted to leave Howard Sommers with some kind of hope, staring down the fires that were closing.

"You're not coming back."

Quinn patted the man's chest, looked back in the direction of Flynn and Boyers, saying, "Said I'm calling for help."

Howard Sommers moved his hand, grimaced though the pain, touched the revolver inside his coat, a Baby Dragoon model. Quinn dropped his hand over his own sidearm. Sliding the revolver onto his belly, Howard checked the load and left it across his stomach, saying, "In case you don't make it back."

Quinn nodded, going back to the top of the side street, thinking he'd yell for Flynn and Boyers, then leave it to them.

. . . DRINK DEEP THE CHRISTIAN WAY

HERE AND there wisps rose from the cinders, what was left of the line of dives along the west side of Stockton. Ramshackle buildings on Powell had been laid flat. A pair of women in ruined dress raised their skirts and stepped, searching through the destruction, ferreting for anything of use. The Melodeon was gone, the building caved in on itself, looking like a giant pile of kindling. Part of an archway was standing where the Concert Saloon had been, at the far end of the block. Nothing much left in between the broken boards and sections of roofing.

This part of Whiting had been shaken, but spared from the sweep of fire. Showing fractures and missing roof shingles, Pearly's Gates stood intact. A fissure ran down the street a dozen feet from its porch steps, wide enough to drop a trolley car into. A ragged split through the Empress Dancehall, from foundation to roof peak; looked like a giant cleaver had split it in two. The framework out of plumb, the structure listing, touching Pearly's at the roofline. The Oasis across the street stood undamaged.

The two drunks Levi and Mack had run into outside St. Anthony's swung near-empty bottles, toting army packs filled with plunder: liquor, tobacco and canned meat. Stopping at the edge of the fissure, Purvis and Hawk stood wide-legged and pissed, arguing with a reservist about serving their fellow man in this time of crisis.

The reservist's hand stayed on the carbine over his shoulder, uneasy about the pistols sticking from their belts, turning his head as the men pissed. The two reeked of booze, looking dirty and dangerous. One wearing a Confederate forage cap, the taller one with a milky eye.

Coming from the direction of the overcrowded camp at Fort Mason, displaced townsfolk shambled past them, carrying or hauling whatever they could, along a constricted path cleared down the center of Whiting.

"So you 'spect me and Hawk to just up and help you, that it?" Purvis asked, drinking from his bottle. "And you ain't gonna pay us?"

"It's your Christian duty," the reservist said, thinking these two smelled worse than the inside of hell's back-house — booze, sweat and smoke in equal measure. Point was, they were able-bodied, and orders were orders: round up any single man able to draw breath, get them back to Fort Mason.

The two men looked at each other, incredulous, drunken laughter. Purvis eyed the carbine, wondering about the contents of the man's pockets, asking the reservist if he had a bite of hardtack or such.

"I brought nothing with me but my orders."

"Well, I ain't never heard of this Funstein you been jawing about," Hawk said, tucking himself in, leaving his trousers unbuttoned, and taking a pull from his bottle, legs wobbling.

"General Funston," the reservist said, catching the man's arm to keep him from tipping into the fissure.

"Understand, son, we put hand to shovel, we get paid to do it," Hawk said. "We're working men, and that's the way of things. Decent wage for a day's work. Ain't that so, Purvis? This volunteering's for plain idiots."

"And Christians," Purvis threw in.

"What's the difference?" Hawk said, the two of them cackling on and toasting their wit, teetering on the edge. Scratching under his reb's cap, Purvis recalled Funston at some rally or other. "A runt of a man," Purvis said, "no bigger than a woman. Fact, heard he learned his generaling from some book, one he never finished reading."

More cackling.

"All I know is I got my orders," the reservist said, unslinging his carbine. "And if you men refuse to comply, then you force me to —"

Drunk or not, Purvis snatched the weapon from the man's grasp, twisting him by the sleeve and yanking him stumbling to the brink. "I'd say that settles things, wouldn't you Hawk?" Purvis turned and walked along the cleared path, adjusting his pack, inspecting his new carbine.

"Best watch your step there, boy," Hawk said, offering the reservist his hand, tugging him from the edge, telling him to have a drink.

The reservist refused the bottle. "Sooner stick my head in a horse trough."

Shrugging, Hawk staggered after Purvis, tipping his bottle.

Dressed in tatters and dragging a suitcase fastened to roller skates, a tall man in a nightshirt bumped past the reservist, causing him to stumble, knocking his cap into the breach. Nightshirt just kept on in the same direction as Hawk and Purvis.

A couple coming behind him shoved a steamer trunk perched on a child's wagon, maneuvering the path, the man saying to the reservist, "Ain't things hard enough without you fools getting in the way."

Stepping out of their path, the reservist watched the drunks walk away with his army-issue carbine, faced with explaining it to his sergeant.

Over the clacking of the child's wagon came a rumble from the south. A blast, not a tremor. The army said to be creating fire lanes somewhere back along Van Ness, detonating blocks of buildings, taking away anything the fires could feed on. The reservist thinking he ought to head down there, see if he could be more useful fighting fires than he was at recruiting men.

•

HAWK AND Purvis didn't recognize Mack Lewis, making room on the path for the man with the child and the trailing women. Fussing with the frock around Emma, the child fast asleep in his arms, Mack was singing the words to the only lullaby he knew. *Sleepyhead, close your eyes, mother's right here beside you.* Not paying any mind to the stumbling drunks passing by.

Angling her shoulders, Mabel passed the men, the oversized clothing Mack absconded with making a sharp contrast to the fashion plate Hawk and Purvis had seen in front of the Mission just two days ago. Hooking her thumb around the denim seam, Mabel kept the trousers up, her feet blistered from sliding around in her torn slippers inside the oversized shoes of stiff leather. Her eyes burning from the smoke and floating debris.

Dead on their feet, Agnes and Verna followed, holding each other up.

Stepping off the path, Purvis tipped his forage cap, winking to the ladies, clinking his bottle against Hawk's, offering a toast, both women refusing a drink.

The two men threw their arms about each other and headed for the waterfront, aiming to go in the opposite direction of the ferry terminal. Taking a fresh bottle from his pack, Purvis tossed the empty in the wreckage and started into "Whiskey for My Johnny," Hawk joining him in no-part harmony. The way they figured it, the entire northwest section was theirs to plunder before the fires came and swallowed it forever.

...THIS MARBLE SHIT

FIRST THE man had gone about looting her something to wear other than night clothes, nearly ended up shot for it. Now Mack brought them to this brothel, the three-story having gone unscathed, the building next to it leaning into this one, another across the street smashed nearly flat.

Mabel sat with Emma on the chaise, happy that the child was sleeping. She looked back down the hallway, the smashed chandelier at the base of the stairs, chunks of ceiling plaster on the floor. Then, looking at this big madam pouring from a jug, Mabel saying, "Thank you." Accepting the tin cup from Pearly and drinking from it, the water wonderful going down her dry throat.

"For the baby," Pearly said, taking her kerchief, offering it to Mabel.

Thanking her again, Mabel couldn't help the glance at the framed photos of near-naked men, trying to hide any feelings about the place.

"Sorry, I haven't got more to offer." Pearly smiled, the pretty blonde looking from the photos, smiling back.

"Water's just fine," Mabel said, both women grinning, then laughing. Dipping a corner in the cup, Mabel wiped it to Emma's lips, drank down the rest of the water, Pearly asking the baby's name, saying she was the spitting image.

"You're very kind," Mabel said, handing back the cup. Pearly pouring more from the jug, handed the tin cup to Agnes, looking to Verna. "Sorry, could only find the one cup."

"Brought my own," Verna said, taking the flask from her pocket, offering it to Pearly.

More laughter.

"Well, now." Pearly taking it, unscrewing the cap, sniffing, a smile of delight, taking a good sip. "Sure hits the spot." Passing it back to Verna.

●

THE WAINSCOTING at the top of the stairs had splayed from the wall, was hanging like clapboard. The marble table was split clean in two. Pearly and Mack stood outside her boudoir door, then stepped around a shattered fixture and back into the hall, Pearly using her hickory handle meant for an axe like a walking stick.

"Well, stranger things have happened on that bed," she said, glancing back into the room. Mabel curled around Emma, Agnes and Verna spooning, sharing the best blanket Pearly could muster. Pearly's Victrola lay smashed on the sitting-room floor. Stubbing her toe on a jagged chunk, she hobbled a step, swiping at it with the handle, grabbing the loose rail. "Goddamn this marble shit."

Coming up the stairs, Woody tested the railing, seeing

if it was steady, giving warning about the shattered chandelier and busted glass at the bottom by the door. Wires dangled from the cracked ceiling, Woody saying, "I been wondering about all the headstones in the cemetery. Ain't they made out of that marble shit, Pearly?" Woody trying to get a glimpse into the boudoir.

"Don't be thinking thoughts like you're going to be thinking, Woody." Stepping to him, Pearly shook a finger. "Just be glad you lived to tell it." Then she took his shoulders and turned him around.

"Guess so," he said.

She said to Mack, "He's been going off like that. You get him started with spooks and ghosts and such, and he never buttons it."

Woody grinned, saying, "I can get awful worked up about it. Had an auntie back in Storyville. Well, wasn't really my —"

Pearly swatted his backside, saying, "Go get worked up about fetching water fit for brewing tea."

"Sure thing, Pearly." Going to the top of the stairs, he stopped. "We got tea?"

"Someplace, I suppose," Pearly said. "Next thing you do when you get back with the water, root around the storeroom for it. I expect the ladies will appreciate a pot once they wake." She guessed milk would be best for the baby, but where the hell would anybody find milk in this beaten part of town, even on a good day?

Nodding, Woody picked his way down the littered stairs.

"Woody's the only one didn't run off," Pearly said. "Yellow heart, but rest of him's true-blue, not like that damned Elmer and them others."

"Got nowhere to run off to, Pearly," Woody called from

below, stepping down and jumping across the chandelier. "And where you suppose I'm gonna find fit tea-making water?"

"Broken main out on Whiting. See it's clear before you fill the jug."

"Yes, ma'am. And what do I put —"

"You rather I tend it myself?" Pearly yelled, leaning over the rail, reeling back, remembering it was loose, watching him go out the door. Turning to Mack, she shook her head like she was dealing with an infant. "You want something done, best tend it yourself."

"Least he stuck around."

"Yeah. Anyway, go on . . . about you two getting locked up."

Mack conveyed getting caught inside Healey's mansion with a sack of plunder while Quinn and Florence were getting biblical upstairs, Pearly laughing at that, wishing she'd been there to see it. Mack telling how it came about, how Levi got away, him and Red Tom getting the cockfight money, Red Tom getting shot, how he and Levi ended in Quinn's jail. "Wasn't looking so good till this hell and brimstone hit."

"Least it did somebody some good," she said, starting down the stairs. "So Quinn fancies you offed his brother on that woman's say-so?"

"Woman sure can act up a storm, tell you that much." He followed.

"Well, a woman's myrtle's a powerful persuader," Pearly said, shaking her head, "especially that one's," laughing, the thought of the Healey woman screwing the copper brother with her husband barely cold after she blew his brains out his ear. High fucking society, white gloves, pinkies straight up from their teacups.

"Getting nabbed with a sack of loot in her front hall didn't exactly pull my way." Mack lifting up his trouser leg, showing the dog bites.

"Guess it didn't." Pearly grinned, shaking her head, making the bottom of the stairs, raising her skirts, ignoring Mack's offered hand, stepping clear of the shattered fixture.

"Any luck, the roof beam sent that son straight to his maker," Mack said, stepping over.

"Amen to that."

"Wouldn't be so bad if the Healey bitch met him, too."

Still smiling, she said, "Whatever Healeys are left will still pull freight in this town. And they'll come for you."

"I know it." Mack finished telling her how Levi had gone after the cockfight money and cans of gold he had buried in the cellar.

"Half thought the Healeys set him up with that story," she said.

"Na-uh. The *Call* claimed thirty thousand in coins went missing from the Mint, chief clerk in on it."

"Believe everything you read?"

"Believe how Levi told it."

"So, why the hell'd you let him go off on his own like that?" She got close, throwing her hands in the air.

"The man's dogged. Plus I had them." Mack glanced up the stairs. "Told me to meet up soon's I finish saving damsels."

"Well, I think you're done with that," Pearly said, didn't need to be told Mack had feelings for the pretty blonde on her bed, the cute little muffin in her arms.

"Levi'll be wanting you to come along, too," Mack said.

"Want all he likes."

"Figured you'd argue, but I got to insist."

"You packing a gun on you?"

He flapped his jacket, showing he didn't.

"Then how would that come about?" Stamping the hickory on the boards, serious, then tweaking his cheek, this woman who'd tossed more than one man from her stoop, saying, "Not going anywhere with my place still standing. You know it. I know it. Every goddamned thing I own's inside these walls."

. . . FRENCH LEAVE

THE SMOKE rolled thick and angry. The last of the rescuers were called in and gathered around the wagon, waiting on the lieutenant's signal, every man anxious to get out of there.

Swarming rats, hundreds of them, some big as cats, ran up the street, ahead of the fires. Volunteers and soldiers kicked at those that got close. Some of the men ran over, trying to keep the rats from the dead at the curbside, the rats just heading for safety.

No time left to tend to the bodies, the roaring loud enough to block any more cries from the Portland House. Waiting as long as he dared, Lieutenant Jinks signaled his sergeant.

It was Booth who saw them first, three men on the rooftop of Crown Forging. Shouting and waving for rescue. The lower floors were alight, allowing no escape, no way down. Flames danced through the upper floor, forcing the three to the edge, leaving them nothing but the choice of being roasted alive or jumping.

Looking for a way to send some men, Jinks looked, hesitating, realizing it was impossible. He told Booth to fetch his best marksmen, the sergeant looking at him, realizing what had to be done, then nodding and calling out two names. All eyes watching, not believing what they were seeing. Booth took a rifle in his own hands, Reverend Thadeus standing, saying words from the wagon bed, knowing what was about to happen.

"At your will, men." Booth took a careful bead and fired. One man was gone. The other two up on the roof just looked and waited. The two soldiers aimed and fired, and the roof was cleared. Everyone looking up a moment longer, Thadeus finishing with a God rest their souls, the fires howling over his words.

Some wept, several crossed themselves, but they all started moving. Jinks ordered the driver to roll on to the Mechanics' Pavilion, a temporary refuge and morgue. Dismounting, he handed the reins to a corporal, told him to ride ahead and scout the best route through the razed streets.

Grey smoke whorled around them, Thadeus hunched in the wagon, his eyes closed, hands in prayer, the lieutenant grabbing hold of the wagon's side, the driver clucking on the team, the frightened horses eager to oblige.

Levi trotted alongside the volunteers and wounded, all of them sullen. The route took them south on Mission, away from the House of Blazes, Levi thinking his brief service to the army was done, timing his French leave.

Abreast of a burned-out streetcar truck, he drifted to the rear of the line, bending to take a stone from his boot, allowing the column to pull away. Darby looked back and gave a nod; Levi waved a hand and slipped on the moccasins, leaving the boots Darby had given him in the street.

Walking and putting the streetcar truck between him and the line of rescuers, Levi cut down the first alley, finding himself at the rear of a wrecked library building, thousands of books turned to ash, some still smoldering. Climbing a hash of tumbled boards, he covered his face with his lapel, unable to block the stench of burning flesh coming from the next block over, Levi guessing a slaughterhouse.

Scaling a twisted fence, he turned between a pair of brick buildings, crossing a railway line, then climbing over a fallen wall papered with advertisements about ready-to-wear hats and ladies' cloaks. The bones of the Duncan Sugar Refinery stood across from an abandoned armory, a Civil War mortar on its torn lawn.

These streets had been evacuated, the fires had swept through. This part of town looked war-ravaged, a fire-hose bundle laid by another abandoned pumper, the firefighters forced away. Felt like walking through hell's blast furnace, heat shimmers rising up from the ground ahead. Unsupported walls and smashed pillars threatened to collapse. Another empty street, a cable car track ripped and twisted like ribbon candy. A body laid curled like it was sleeping, featureless like a mannequin, skin blackened and crusting.

Picking his way along an iron skeleton, making it to the highest point, Levi looked at what he guessed was to be the Fairmont in the distance. The *Chronicle* had boasted how she was near completion, ranking her among the finest of hotels. Soon to be the pride of San Francisco. The fires appeared heavier up ahead. He couldn't see a way through it or around it. Climbing down, he made his way back to the cable car tracks, the heat blistering now. Throwing an arm in front of his face, he retreated a block before turning south.

Getting around an adobe wall, he found some shelter from the heat. Then Levi was back out front of the tannery, the road ahead barricaded by fallen brick. Turning into another lane, he stumbled onto the old man Quinn had left pinned under the steel girder. Looking at the man's crushed legs, Levi took him for dead, reaching for the pistol on the man's belly.

. . . TEMPEST

HALF THE plaster from the ceiling lay in chunks along the hall, lath exposed like ribs. Photographs smashed and scattered about the parlor.

"Get on, then," Pearly told Mack, giving him a tap with the hickory handle, then leaning on it, saying, "They'll be fine. And that fire's got about all it's getting."

Mack said again it didn't feel right just leaving them.

"I'll keep an eye, and I got Woody. Talk is the soldiers got another camp going up at the Presidio. They'll come rounding folks up with promises of food and water. And that's more than you can do."

She was right. Mack needed to go find Levi.

She was set to swat at him again, not liking that Levi was out there on his own, saying, "Goddamn it, Mack. They look in terrible danger sleeping on my bed?"

"Not so much."

"Well, I ain't open for business, case you're thinking this house ain't a fitting place for such fine ladies with a child."

"It's not that."

"That skinny thing and her baby need the rest. Nothing more to be done. And you need to get on and find Levi. That man's got more ways of getting in jackpots than he has for getting out." Swatting again.

"I'm going." Mack stepped for the door.

Woody rushed up the steps, bumping into him, eyes wide, flapping his hands like he was trying to take flight.

"What the hell's got you now?" Pearly said. "And where's my tea water?"

"He's struck the match." Woody flapped, kept up the epileptics, pointing out the door.

"Who did?"

"That Blake. He's burning down the Empress." Grabbing Mack by the arm, Woody dragged him out and down the steps, Pearly hurrying behind.

●

IN THE street, in his sackcoat and vest, Byron Blake looked up at the Empress, his life's work. There was more than enough in the trunk to start again. He'd been thinking of setting up a righteous bookshop back east, though the blustering cold of the Eastern Seaboard, where he grew up, held little appeal for him, as did the bedside of his ailing mother, the woman suffering from an irritable bowel, her doctor called it. Made him smile, picturing her headstone: *Here lies Margaret Eloise Blake, died of the quick step.* That woman always had that damned beanpot cooking; the locals loved to spout, "You don't know beans till you come to Boston."

Fuck Boston.

Lived there long before the fires took that town, wiping out his first bookshop with the apartment above it, the reason he came out west in the first place, to start over.

Now this.

Sloshing the bucket of fuel down, he tucked the knees of his trousers, adjusted the pistol in his belt and sat on his steamer. Wiping his specs on a shirttail, he watched the upper windows, the flames spreading to the curtains. Could hear it, sounded like someone was crunching paper, snapping twigs, the fire consuming everything inside.

Now, he'd end up walking Beantown streets again, older, but this time with money, spinning a watch chain and tipping his hat to the dames of society politely farting in their bloomers.

Yeah, fuck Boston.

Promised his best whores, Vilvie and Pomela, they had a future at Byron Blake Booksellers — been with him since day one, the pair standing next to his steamer, watching the place go up, each with the sum of their lives in the carpet bags at their feet. He imagined these two working in a bookshop, sure neither of them could read. Likely offer the gents a free humdinger with every sizable purchase.

Both were clever enough to know the man had no intention of it, just needed a hand with his steamer. Help him get it on a ferry and he'd shake them at the first whistle stop. Leave them high and dry. Just the way Byron Blake was. The man not long on sentiment.

Byron watched Mack come out of Pearly's, looking at the flames shooting through the upper windows of the Empress and threatening Pearly's. Mack ran past Pearly, going back inside, leaping over the chandelier, yelling Mabel's name, taking the stairs two at a time.

Turning his eyes to the fire, Byron didn't see Pearly barrel down the steps, pushing past Woody. Storming around the crater, she headed for him, gripping the hickory handle, calling, "Goddamn you, Blake, you gone fucking loco?"

Byron pointed to the rip over his front door, running all the way to the roof. It was explanation enough.

"You set your own fucking house on fire?" she said, wagging the handle.

"Insurance company won't pay no earthquake damage," he said, liking her all riled, ignoring the weapon, the woman all talk.

"So you figured lighting up the place would fix things?"

"Only got insurance against fire." He waved a hand, meaning what else was there to do.

An upper window burst, its glass hailing down, smoke pluming from one of the bedrooms, flames reaching like fingers, sparks drifting to Pearly's roof.

"Still, not easy to watch it all go to hell," he said, looking up.

A second window burst, more sparks jumping out, Pearly pointing up with the handle, his rooftop touching hers, yelling at him, "You stop to think my place is going to catch, same as yours?"

"Like I said, insurance . . ." Without Hayes or Lewis to back her, what could she do? "Look around you, Wilkes. This city's going to hell, case you didn't notice." Liking the way her color changed, the look in her eyes, getting to her, saying, "And why not your fucking place? Hell, ought to thank me, insurance'll build you a new one. So stop your crowing."

She slapped the handle into her palm, eyes boring into him, Byron letting her see the pistol tucked in his belt.

His two whores watched, Vilvie and Pomela sensing what was coming.

The clapboard front of the Empress was charring black, its paint peeling and starting to curl. Refugees in the street stepped off the narrow path, getting away from the blistering heat and embers floating down. The near wall of Pearly's was catching now, the narrow alley between the two buildings alive with dancing flame.

"I got no goddamn insurance," Pearly said, kicking her toe at the dirt. Nothing she could do to stop it.

Byron looked at her, couldn't help laughing, turning to Vilvie and Pomela. "This fucking city's burned to the ground, what, five, six times at least in your day." He turned back to her. "Ask me, you ought to know better." Byron pointed to the flames spreading along Pearly's shingles, making their way to the roof peak. "You got to be dumber than stone not making provisions." Turning back to his whores, he said, "Hear that, girls? The woman's got no insur—"

Snagging him by the collar, Pearly jerked him close, the handle jammed up under his throat, the strength of a man, spit at the corners of her mouth, eyes wild, like she was rabid, saying, "Then I'm having your insurance money."

"The hell you are." One hand gripping the handle pressing at his throat, he tried to jerk free, his other hand reaching for his pistol. Pearly pressed up with the handle, had Byron up on tiptoes, the man letting go of the pistol, both hands at the handle.

"You're paying for every goddamn stick." Outweighing him by a solid thirty pounds, Pearly pressed the hickory, one hand finding his pistol and tossing it in the wreckage.

"Fuck you and your sticks, Wilkes," he said, twisting to free himself, coughing, surprised by her strength. Driving a knee up into her crotch, Byron sucked for air and stepped back, hand at his throat. Wasn't the first woman he'd struck in his day.

She bent to the pain, Byron reaching for his pistol. "And you won't see a penny, and I'm glad to be done with you. Glad to see your shithole burning."

Byron turned to Vilvie and Pomela, saying, "Guess it's time we get —"

Pearly came up swinging the handle, catching the pistol, knocking it away.

"Fuck!" Byron shook the hand, then raised his fists, saying, "Got this coming . . ." And he went at her.

A band of knockabouts, one in a militia jacket, sensed some sport to the fight, stopping from making their way to the waterfront, setting their rifles and packs down, watching the scene unfold, money exchanging hands. Woody moving away from them, hoping to get to the pistol.

"Never been one to strike a woman, 'less I got cause . . ." Byron said, playing to the crowd now.

The man in the militia jacket whooped, a fistful of dollars in his hand, calling out, "Say two-to-one on the woman with the wood."

Two of the men taking the bet.

Byron smiled and aimed a finger at the men, saying, "Smart bet. Wouldn't mind taking some of —"

Spitting, Pearly stepped and swung, knocking Byron back over his steamer, Vilvie and Pomela catching him, helping him like cornermen, pushing him back into the fray. The group of men hooting, more money changing hands: two-to-one on the big woman. Byron getting back into his stance, fists raised the way he remembered John L. Sullivan doing it.

"That cause enough?" Pearly said, winding up the handle.

Tired and dirty, some of the crowd moved on; others coming along set their belongings down, backing from the heat, two whorehouses in flames, the street as bright as a sunny day, pimp versus madam out front dueling. More money was turned out of pockets, wagers laid down.

Everything she owned was being consumed, just like that, clothes from Paris, furniture from London, the Victrola and her savings and jewelry in the strongbox under the bed. Escaping the earthquake only to be ruined by this pantywaist.

Swiping a hand across his bleeding mouth, prudence giving way to rage, Byron flew at her, his fists like knobs. Blocking her swing, catching her blindside, Byron jabbed and hooked, punching her ribs, her gut, grabbing hold of the handle, throwing a hook at her face, jabbing at the tits. Her hair wild and in her eyes. Caught her low with a straight right, and she sagged under it. He flung aside the handle. Didn't bother him a lick, beating this woman, mannish and big-boned, her fists coming up again, begging him for more. Had hated her for years, and this beating was long overdue. Made Byron feel good to do it.

None of the crowd stepped in, money and bottles passing back and forth on the path. Woody moved for the pistol, Vilvie and Pomela grabbing it from him, pressing him between them, each holding an arm, keeping him out of it.

Blood dripping from her mouth, Pearly ducked under the next swing and came in, raking his face, feeling peels of flesh under her nails, ripping his specs away. Kicking and punching, staggering him. Past the pain and more than game now, she swung a haymaker, striking him full on, the nose snapping, blood pouring from both nostrils. The next one put Byron on his ass. Dazed.

Whoops and more money passing — three-to-one now — Byron being mocked, the wind knocked from him, his face bloodied, his nose broken. No woman ever fought him with fists.

Vilvie and Pomela were enjoying this, remembering the times Byron had taken his belt to them. They held Woody fast between them.

Getting his feet under him, Byron hawked up spit and came in fast, going for the tackle. The toe of her shoe stopping him, his gut exploding with pain. Bug-eyed and gasping, he went down on a knee.

The front window of the Empress blew out, more glass raining in the street, fragments of flaming curtains floating around them. Catching a fistful of his hair, Pearly lined him up, driving up her knee, then dropping the point of her elbow like a spike on his spine, flattening him. Pearly put hands on her knees, panting, soaked in sweat.

No specs, Byron gasped — a fish on a dock — swiping grit from his face, choking back the bile. No woman did this to him. Hand going for the razor in the sleeve of his boot, kept there for unruly drunks.

Back on her feet, Pearly came stomping in, trying to gore him with her heels, Byron rolling clear, the crowd wanting blood like a Roman mob. Cumbersome and winded, she kept after him, slamming her feet down, the crowd yelling for her to finish it, the Empress engulfed, the roof beam sagging, past saving. Pearly's upper floor showed flames licking up the siding, smoke puffing from its soffits.

Woody broke free of Vilvie and Pomela and ran back around the fissure and jumped to Pearly's door, yelling for Mack, the heat pushing him back, the place going up like it was made of paper. Through the smoke, he heard the coughing, Mack herding the women down the flights of stairs, Pearly's strongbox under his arm.

Stopping at the smashed chandelier, Woody took the bawling child from Mabel and hurried back out the door, past the fractured earth, pushing through the mob, over to the steps of the Oasis, the place intact but abandoned.

Wallpaper bubbled and curled, flames making the place daylight bright. Mack was the last one out, sucking in air, seeing what was happening in the street.

Byron circled and swung the razor, promising to slit the bitch from one hole to the next. Pearly crouched, chest heaving, adrenalin driving her. Both houses were burning and crumbling behind her, all eyes on the fight.

Pushing through the men, Mack handed Woody the strongbox, ran toward the fight, yelling for Pearly to stop, blindsided, catching the butt end of a rifle, his skull erupting. He went down.

"First bit of fun we had," the one in the militia jacket said, warning him to stay down, another one swinging a kick at his ribs.

Byron slashed, missing with the backswing. Clouting him, Pearly put him down on one knee again. She gave it everything, Byron's false teeth knocked from his mouth. Grinding her foot on the denture, teeth spilling like corn kernels.

Swinging the razor, not much behind it, Byron laid open her calf, Pearly dropping on him and pinning the hand, bulldogging him. Getting on top, she got a grip on the hand with the razor and twisted it free.

Byron screamed, a bloody maw with no teeth, his nose flattened.

Catching hold of his belt, she jerked at his trousers,

pressing her weight down, scrabbling with her legs, staying on top. She clawed the ground and had the razor.

Drawing last reserves, Byron flopped from side to side. Knowing he was finished.

Mack took a punch getting up, the one in the militia jacket swinging down, a second man jumping in, both landing punches, Woody leaving the strongbox with the women, running in and yelling for them to stop. Mack was punching back, taking the worst of it, knocked back to the gap in the earth.

Pearly cut Byron again, the crowd urging her to finish him.

Knocked down, Mack grabbed a fistful of gravel and put weight behind his punch, slugging the one in the jacket. Snatching a carbine from a pile, Woody aimed it at the next man, his eyes wide, looking crazed enough to shoot, jabbing the air with the barrel, the men backing off, leaving their belongings, turning back the way they came.

Mack grabbed another carbine and dumped it into the hole, yelling to Woody, "Shoot anybody you don't like." Then running to the fight.

Woody saying he didn't like any of them, sighting down the barrel, the men backing away, Woody prompting with the carbine.

Rushing into the fight, Mack yanked Pearly off Byron.

"Just being neighborly is all, Mack," Pearly said, spitting blood, kicking a heel at Byron. The woman hurt all over, but she had bested him, beat him to a bloody mess. She turned to Pearly's Gates, the place in ruins, its sign over the peak tumbling down.

Pomela and Vilvie ministered to Byron, easing him onto his steamer, Vilvie pressing a kerchief against a gash on his thigh, Pomela dabbing at his face, guessing they'd be getting on the train alone.

Trouble breathing, Byron felt the heat, saw the squad of soldiers coming from past Stockton and taking charge. The Empress was collapsing inward; Pomela and Vilvie lifted him, wanting to move him farther from it.

Shaking them off, he reeled on his feet, saying, "*Now you bitches want to help?*" Hobbling past his steamer, he reached the bucket of gasoline, soldier running past him, one taking the rifle from Woody. The man in the militia jacket backed over to the women standing by the strongbox, the three of them hugging each other, eyes on Byron, none paying attention to the box by their feet.

Faltering, Byron moved and threw the bucket, washing Pearly in gasoline. Sparks from the sign catching the torn dress. Pearly swatting at it, screaming.

Byron swung the bucket at her, Mack jumping at him, tearing it away, swinging it and knocking him down.

Dress turned to a fireball, Pearly screamed and tried to run from it. Mack ripped off his jacket, ran after her, swatting at her, one of the soldiers doing the same.

Whirling, Pearly shoved by them, Byron trying to crab away from her, screaming. Pearly dropped on him and hugged him tight. Nothing Mack or the soldier could do.

. . . STEELING

FLICKERS DANCED inside the foundry. Could be a blind alley, as hot as a smelting furnace. Timbers tumbled down, sparks flashing from the knocked-out panes. Searching the ground, Levi shoved at broken boards, freeing an iron rod. Swinging it against the wall, he knocked away chunks of concrete. Not sure why, he stopped, this man looking like he had a foot in the grave.

Howard Sommers cried out, Levi leveraging the rod under the beam, telling the old man to hold on, pressing his weight down. The ground giving way a bit, broken-up concrete starting to shift. A board snapped, Levi jabbing the iron around, searching for purchase.

Catching on something solid, he pressed his weight again, the beam stirring. Raising it, he pushed it off. His feet slid on the broken ground as the beam swung clear.

Soaking wet in an instant, Levi fought through the muzziness. "What say we get you out of here?" Tucking

Howard's revolver in his own belt, Levi propped the old man up, hoisting him, Howard crying at the pain.

"Sorry about that," Levi said, getting his balance, the man heavier than he looked. Under the weight, he stepped across the broken ground, deliberate and careful, knowing if he went down, he'd be done, no way he could lift Howard again. The end of the alley lay ahead, looked like it turned left. A pane reflecting their image, the tower of hell closing behind them, flames showing over the building tops. Wouldn't mind seeing Jinks and his rescuers coming back down that street.

Sounded like whispers, the crackling within that roar, like phantoms in the smoke, curling fingers reaching for him. Rising high and pushing the smoke above the flattened city. The grey blocking out the sun.

Barely enough space between the pair of walls, Levi angled and passed through, the building on his right making an L turn around the one on the left. Fear of walking into a blind alley gripped him, flames licking from another busted window, the whispers saying he wouldn't make it.

Picking his way along, using the wall for balance, he felt his thighs ache, legs shaking under the weight. Sucking down hot air, he focused on his steps, turning the corner. The street opened ahead.

A rag doll and tricycle lay at the mouth of the alley. Stepping into the street, Levi thought the cistern of water was a mirage. Half-bending to it and scooping, he held his hand up to Howard's mouth. Spilling most of it. Doing it again. The old man licking at it.

Drinking some, Levi pressed up and moved into the street, not exactly sure where he was, thought he caught sight of someone fleeing ahead of him. Unable to call out.

Shifting Howard's weight on his shoulders, he told himself, steel yourself and you'll make it. Heading for where he thought the ferry building was, staying to the middle of the deserted street, watching his steps.

. . . MAKING IT

A SIDE street of damaged flats opened to the ruins of a school. The ground under the foundation looked liquefied, some of the chimney tumbled down. A group of men stood assessing the damage, official-looking in their suits and bowlers, one hailing to Quinn to come lend a hand, Quinn saying he'd be of no help, showing the splinted arm, saying again he was on a mission for Schmitz, the mayor.

"Still got the one arm," one of the men insisted. "Won't keep you long. And Schmitz be damned."

Drawing his pistol, Quinn guessed it served as answer, walking past a ruptured sewer and an upturned carriage, a fire squad pulling their chemical engine along Kearney.

Heading west on Stockton, Quinn passed a line of injured waiting outside a makeshift hospital, some standing, some sitting, a nurse in white cuffs and apron tending to them, passing out tins of water. A sentry sat posted out front of

St. Louis Brewery, eyes on Quinn and the pistol still in his hand. The two men nodding at each other, their eyes wary.

Burr's Mustard Mill, Bach's Malts, Merle's Plating, all showed damage from the quake, but none of it heavy, and none touched by fire.

Quinn could make out the gantry above the tin rooftops, the Healey Shipbuilding stack, this part of town escaping most of the shake-up and all of the fire, up till now. Crates had been set up at North Point like table and chairs. A makeshift kitchen next to it. Belongings lay out in the street, scarcely a soul around. Quinn guessing the refugees had moved to the ferry docks or been taken to one of the camps.

. . . CAMP GRATEFUL

DOWNSLOPE, THE scattered fires continued to consume what they could of the city, smoke rising from hundreds of ruins out beyond Van Ness. Chimneys stuck up like tombstones, blackened above outlines of foundation walls, the acrid smell hanging in the air.

A squad of cavalry hunched over their saddles, escorting an open farm wagon of the miserable and lost, coming along Presidio Avenue and into the reservation. Mack sat on a bale, tending his bruises and cuts, Mabel and Woody on either side of him. Head in his hands, Woody tried exchanging remembrances of Pearly, Mack preferring to sit quiet, refraining from saying anything about Pearly' missing strongbox, the one he gave Woody to watch.

Upright and asleep, Verna Culp held the empty flask between her knees, Agnes's head in her lap. A middle-aged couple sat stone-faced on the opposite bale, both looking down at the boards. A man with a paunch and singed hat stared downslope at the Armageddon showing through patches of smoke. Arm around his tow-headed boy, the boy asleep against him.

The corporal driving was Hegg — blond, with a lantern jaw, broad in the shoulders. Turning the wagon onto a furrowed field, Hegg passed a row of crates, relief supplies, sacks filled with loaves, cases of preserves, meats, more sacks of potatoes and onions. Jostling the occupants, the wagon slipped into the rutted tracks worn in the grass, Hegg driving the team into the Presidio encampment for the homeless and injured. Looked like hundreds of army tents standing in rows. Aid workers unpacked supplies of food and medicines beyond a charcoal-scrawled sign dubbing this Camp Grateful.

A group of a dozen girls, led in song by a wizened choir master, lent harmony to "Bringing In the Sheaves," singing they'd come rejoicing. Whitewash on a splintered board declared them the Presbyterian Mission Choir. This being their temporary digs, the girls doing their part to bring comfort.

Woody lifted his eyes to the singing, the distant rumbling coming from downslope. "When it first struck," he said, poking Mack to get him looking, "sounded like an ore car rolling down the mine shaft of hell."

"Don't start up again, Woody, for Christ's sake, please . . ." Mack said, then apologized to the stone-faced couple for the profanity.

"I was in an elevator that hit the sheaves one time," the man with the singed hat said, looking over at Woody.

"That so?" Woody said, jumping when the man punched his open palm.

The man saying, "Felt just like that."

Woody nodding.

Verna looked at the man, Singed Hat saying he was

sorry, noting the flask, guessing it was empty, taking out his own hip flask, holding it out to her, saying, "Helps take the edge off what you been through, am I right, ma'am?"

He was forgiven, Verna lit up and reached, giving him a smile. "Why, you sure are, sir."

Another rumble sounded, curious faces turning, looking downslope.

"What is that god-awful thunder?" Mabel asked Corporal Hegg.

"Army's blowing up buildings in the path of the fire, ma'am," he said. "Calling it 'fire lanes.'"

Mack noted the corporal looking at her longer than he needed.

"What on earth for?" Mabel asked, fussing with Emma.

"Need to make the lanes, see, ma'am. On account the water mains are all busted, water towers and pumpers all useless. It's all there's for anybody to do."

"But destroying more buildings . . ." It didn't make sense to her.

"Only way to stop it, ma'am — take away what it feeds off," Hegg said, his eyes sweeping across her, the ill-fitting clothes.

She nodded, not so sure, tugging the collar of the shirt to her neck.

"They been springing buildings all around the Mint since early this morning," Singed Hat said, "so's to save it. Don't know whether they did much saving, but they sure was trying all they could. Damnedest sight to see — those sworn to protect, blowing everything to hell."

Hegg turned and gave the man a look, then turned back and clucked his team.

"City of the Golden West, my aunt Fanny's knickers,"

Verna said, enough vexation to draw looks from the others. Tipping the flask, then handing it back to Singed Hat. Her smile said thanks, Singed Hat toasting her health, having some himself.

"City Hall's nothing but a picked carcass," the stone-faced man said. "Just the dome sitting on its bones, least it was this morning. Ain't that so, mate woman?"

Bobbing her head, the wife took an apple from her pocket, polishing it and holding out her empty hand.

Stone-Face ignored her, telling the others about the six-foot-wide crack in the ground over by the Valencia Hotel, speculating that the damned thing ran straight to the core of the Earth, maybe to hell itself.

Woody drew a breath.

"The teeth, Horace," his wife insisted with a nudge, saying, "you know I can't muff no apple."

Cupping a hand over his mouth, Stone-Face popped out the teeth, passed them to her.

Setting them in place, the woman wiggled her jaw; then, reaching a folding knife, she cut a wedge of apple, looking up, everyone watching her. Offering the slice around, she said, "Only way I can eat it." Her grin showing the ill-fitting teeth.

Some smiled. Woody reached in and thanked her for the slice, shoving it in his mouth.

Hegg rolled them past a breadline more than a hundred souls long. Hollow eyes looking up at the wagonload of smiling fools. Corporal Hegg halting his team by the quartermaster's tent, the tent shaped like a teepee.

The horseback soldiers rode on in single file, heading down the center of a double line of dingy army tents, hooves flipping up clumps of mud. A clothesline of fluttering sheets spanned the gap between two of the tents, the sheets dipping and brushing along the muddy ground.

Cooking fires tended by soldiers in shirtsleeves, the men fixing coffee and soup, passing tins to the homeless standing in wait. Wooden casks lined outside the quartermaster's tent, branded flour, sugar, oatmeal and coffee. One soldier with a Rip Van Winkle beard relaxed atop the one marked coffee, whistling and tapping his heels against the wood, his rifle across his lap. Dozens of townsfolk milled around, hovering over their steaming tins, clutching them like they were lifegiving. Someone playing a mouth organ, a mournful tune on his G harp. Another man singing some words, humming the ones he didn't know.

Hegg hopped from the wagon seat, offering a hand to the ladies, Verna, then Agnes, the middle-aged woman, taking his time with Mabel and Emma, telling all of them cooking fires weren't allowed. "Quartermaster'll get you fixed up with a tent and food and water." Saying to Mabel, "Head cook's a fellow goes by Max, a craggy German codger, but he makes pretty fair chowder and biscuits to go along." Pointing at the tent. "Tell him I sent you by, he'll be sure to get real milk for your child." Hegg smiled when she thanked him, watching her walk to the quartermaster's.

Losing the charm, he looked to the men, saying they best keep to camp tonight, calling them gents. Eyes on Mack, he said, "Army's got a strict curfew, and I'd sure hate for any of you fellows to be mistaken for looters. Army's got strict orders to fire on any man even looking the wrong way, and not to worry too much about any questions after." He patted his sidearm as he spoke.

. . . IN CLOVER

THE HOUSE of Blazes stood at Battery and Whiting, listing against the Arson and Lace, both absconded by the Healeys. Both taverns would have tumbled or turned turtle if they weren't propping each other up. Siding boards were snapped, both doors knocked from their hinges, windows shattered, both tin roofs looking like they'd been buckled by a giant hand. Flames showed to the south, held back by the breeze coming off the Bay.

Quinn gauged the inferno might just miss this section if the breeze pushed to the west. Didn't really matter. Outside of what was bequeathed to him, he didn't much give a shit for the shipyard one way or the other. Not one lost to nostalgia and sentiment.

The door lay on the ground. Drawing his pistol, he slipped inside, getting out of the light in case Hayes or Lewis had got here ahead of him. Patting his way along the wall, he let his eyes adjust to the dark, his ears sharp.

Only the creak from the floorboards under him, the flap of a pigeon settling in the rafters. Crossing in front of the staircase, he stopped along the line of crates, listening some more. The patter of a rat over his boot, Quinn moving along the bar, looking everywhere but down, barely missing the open trapdoor again.

Passing the workbench, he pressed the pistol under his arm, the lids off the casks the way he'd left them. The silhouette of Red Tom over by the wall where he'd died. Fumbling inside the first one, Quinn felt for the satchels. He told the dead Indian he intended to spend it in good health. Looking around, he wondered again where in hell Hayes had hid the coins, had to be in here someplace. He'd searched the place more than once looking for them: been through every room, checked for loose boards, tapped every wall for the hollow sound of a hidden compartment.

He'd consider it some more while he waited for them to show. With the little light coming from the window in the upstairs hall, Quinn rewrapped his wrist, smiling, thinking of Florence and the things she did to him, that carnal hunger, his brother barely gone.

. . . EMBARCADERO

FIRST TIME the sun poked through the heavy shroud. For those waiting, it felt like a song of hope. Two ironclad fire-boats, the *Flyer* and the *Ernestina*, blasted their geysers of water, arching the spray over the rooftops along the water-front. Both fire companies worked their water cannons, soaking everything within reach. For now, they were holding it back, the mist cooling the air, welcomed by the line of folks waiting for the rescue boats.

Dock workers cast off their lines; another ferry laden with refugees underway for Oakland. Workers scrambled, waving their arms, cueing the next boat to the dock. Using the piers not lost to the quake, Pier Five in ruins, Three and Seven on either side untouched. Every manner of craft floated in the Bay, waiting to take a boatload across, Oakland dubbed the Haven of Hope.

A fire chief's horse-drawn buggy, its insignia on the side, red wheels and red seat, raced up along East Street and stopped out front of a makeshift hospital tent across from the Depot. A doctor and an orderly jumped out, carrying a woman on a stretcher past the tent flaps. A fireman climbed down cradling an injured boy in his arms, ushering his crying sister inside.

A few of Lieutenant Jinks's squad leaned against the damaged Depot wall, the men exhausted, coffee tins in their hands. Some sat against the wall, their heads bobbing on their chests, legs stretched out on the walkway, men and uniforms black from soot. The post of keeping peace at the docks had been handed down, Jinks's men ordered to fire on any man jumping onto the rescue ships out of turn.

The corporal's name was Redding, and he took up the watch, letting his men rest, ignoring the bottle passing from man to man, pouring a splash into their tins. Redding thinking if any man ever deserved whiskey, it was any one of his squad. Shoving and panic in the line had been sporadic, his men breaking up a number of fights, mostly men who had lost everything, some of them drunk, not wanting to wait on rescue. Three men and a woman had drowned earlier in the day trying to jump onto the rescue boats, falling or shoved between the hulls and pilings.

Nobody as yet had been shot for jumping the line, Redding hoping to keep it that way. His conscience weighed heavy enough for retreating from the Portland House, knowing there were still people trapped inside. Standing by while Jinks ordered the three men shot from the rooftop. Not faulting his officer, just something that would stay with him all his days.

By noon, the fires had burned low or were quieted by the fireboats along this stretch, and most people in line were too weary to do more than stand or sit on packs and wait to board.

Putting his back to a column, the weariness in his legs, Redding sipped the mud-for-coffee some civilian had handed him — chicory, he guessed by its taste. Exchanging the occasional word, he wished the folks Godspeed as they milled past, sorry-looking, carrying their bundles along with the weight of the world, some dragging trunks, queueing to get to safety. Some asked how long a wait, a young mother with her baby wrapped in a tablecloth wanted to know about food and shelter on the far side.

Redding settled his eyes on the firemen battling a blaze a block over on Mission, the fire beyond the fireboats' range. The squad working the single hydrant that was still pumping water. At it for the past hour, standing their ground, appearing as silhouettes against the glow coming from inside the structure, the building reduced to an iron skeleton, interior walls and roof cladding gone. Looked like they'd had it licked, but now the fire was feeding off a new breeze, threatening to spread. The firemen relieving each other on the hose, spraying down the neighboring walls, laboring in the choking air, refusing to give an inch of ground.

Finishing the mud in his cup, he caught sight of a lone figure coming up Market. At first, he figured it was just another tottering drunkard, trudging under a duffel. The man barely on his feet, swaying side to side. As he neared Third, Redding saw it wasn't a duffel that he balanced across his shoulders.

. . . SAINTS AND SINNERS

LEVI'S STRIDES had become mechanical, his muscles long past feeling the aches. Not looking up now, not wanting to see how far, he just stepped in the direction of the water. Made his way along Folsom, catching a glimpse of the Call Building over at Third and Market, the flames still at work, smoke swirling around its top floors. Hardly passed a soul, nobody moving to help. The smoke became lighter; a tumbled wall forced him to cut over to Howard. Levi getting himself over to Market, turning for the water, making it past Main, past Spear, one foot in front of the other, getting away from the heat, his skin feeling like it had burned and peeled from his back. Steeling himself to make it, he fixed his mind on the old times up on the American River, him and Pap panning for gold. Levi remembering the feel of the icy waters, running his pan and sifting.

No idea how Howard Sommers was. No sound from the

man, the man just a sagging weight. Hoping he'd just passed out.

Levi didn't hear the footfalls, didn't see the soldiers coming on the double. Many hands easing the old man from him, lowering him onto a stretcher. Somebody handing Levi water. The sudden weightlessness brought on his own weariness. Levi hung onto the need to get to the coins, drinking the water, saying, "Out of my way . . . get to the Blazes . . ." trying to focus, but sheer exhaustion came up in a rush, spinning him into the dark.

... EGGS AND HAM AND A BLACK HOLE

SLEEP HAD been fitful; strange voices on the edge of consciousness brought him around. Mack was thinking of Mabel Porter. Maybe he'd been dreaming of her. Opening his eyes, Mack focused on the roof of the tent. Musty-smelling and yellowed.

There was no Mabel, only his worn boots next to him, no snoring coming from Woody's cot. Hoping the fool hadn't wandered into more shit outside the encampment, recalling Hegg's warning. Grasping the center pole, he righted himself and poked his head through the flap, the acrid stench from the fires weaker now, giving way to that of bacon and coffee. Stepping out, he swiped a hand through hair thick with ash. Sitting in front of the tent, he stuck a boot on a foot, then the other.

Accepting a tin of boiled eggs and biscuit and another of coffee from a passing padre, he said yeah, there were two more boys in the tent, gave a thanks, set the extra plates inside the flap, the padre wishing him a good day, shoving his handcart to the next tent, the ground rough and muddy under its wheels.

Peeling the shells. The first of the eggs went down like the best thing he ever ate; he washed two more down with the brew, not hot, not good, but welcome. He'd be the one to tell Levi about Pearly, thinking about that now, always wondered if the two had seen some history after his old man was gone. Mack thinking he should have stayed with Levi in case Quinn made it from under the fallen station house.

Peeling another egg, he tried pushing off thoughts of Pearly and Byron dying like that. Looking around the city of tents, people moving along the muddy row between them, some sitting, some lying in the open with nothing to cover them. Boxes, packs and piled belongings next to them. Not enough tents to go around.

Woody spared him from the black hole, coming from the direction of the quartermaster's tent, carrying a whole ham under an arm, a tin of coffee in his free hand. Squatting and twanging the support rope like a banjo string, humming "Everlasting Arms." Gulping a mouthful, Woody looked at the plate of eggshells, setting the ham on the grass. Mack reaching inside the tent, taking one of the plates, handing it to him.

"Got salt?" Woody asked, getting a blank look. Shrugging, he peeled an egg and took it in a single bite, a soldier in an ill-fitting uniform rolling a wagon wheel along one of the ruts, looking doubtful at the two men and the ham.

"As a young'un, I couldn't stomach the whites," Woody said, his cheek full of egg, watching the man pass.

"That so?" Mack said, eyeing the ham.

"Then for a while, it was the yellows I couldn't abide."

Finishing the other egg and biscuit, Woody drew his folding knife, took the ham on his lap and shaved a slice, folding it into his mouth.

"What whites and yellows you talking about?" Mack asked.

"Eggs."

Accepting a slice, Mack sniffed it, guessing it was alright.

"Always seemed squidgy," Woody said. "Guess things change by and by. Eat 'em now every chance I get."

"How you come by it?" Mack pointed his tin at the ham.

"From a feller I slept next to over by the supply tent."

Mack asking what he was doing sleeping over there.

"When you started sawing logs something fiercesome, I went stretching my legs." Woody shrugged, passing another shaving off his blade. "Met a fellow had a jug, sitting with the ham fellow. The two of them didn't mind me being colored, sharing what they had." He patted the ham. "Helped them eat and drain that bark juice, then guess I just nodded off." Woody wiped the knife in the grass. "Come morning, the jug fellow was gone, and the ham fellow's sleeping, except with no breath coming out of him."

"He was dead?"

"Must've been called up." Woody pointed the blade skyward, saying, "Lying there all peaceful with the ham in his arms."

Mack stopped chewing.

"Could be all this was just too much for him," Woody said, shaving another slice. "Sure gives a fellow something to think on, him alive one minute and not so much the next, eyes as glazed as this ham." Offering it to Mack.

Waving it off, Mack spit what he was chewing into his palm, flicked it past the side of the tent. He reached inside the flap, took the last plate, offered Woody an egg.

"Ham's perfectly fine. I just figured the fellow was done with it . . ." Woody taking an egg, helping himself to the biscuit.

"How much of it he eat, this dead fellow?"

"Man didn't die of no ham," Woody said. "I ate more than him, and I'm in the pink." Another slice going in his mouth, Woody saying the ham man looked well-to-do to top it off. "Gold watch, fine suit of clothes, no worse for wear."

"Let's see the watch," Mack said, nodding at Woody's pockets.

Looking sheepish, Woody slipped a finger in his inside pocket, showed the timepiece and chain. "Guess in a mess like this, being well-to-do don't mean much."

"Guess not."

A mother walked past, leading her young girl by the hand, heading for the quartermaster's, the same soldier with the long beard napping on the coffee cask, his rifle across his lap. The girl saying she wanted to go home.

"Hush child, there's no home to go to," the mother said, tugging her along.

Getting up, tucking away the timepiece, Woody swiped his hands on his pant legs, calling to the woman, "My friend and I done ate our fill of this fine ham, ma'am. Fact, if I take so much as another bite . . ." He tapped his stomach, holding the ham out to her. "We'd be happy for you and your young'un to have it."

Looking doubtful, the woman accepted the unwrapped ham, saying, "That's very kind and decent, mister."

"Oh, I ain't a mister," Woody said, "but it's glazed just the same."

"Glazed is best," the woman agreed, her smile tight, mindful not to touch the ham against her greyed dress. The child turned and followed, the woman heading back the way she came.

"Why'd that darkie give us meat, Momma?" the girl asked.

"Hush child, likely snuck it from the supply tent. But we come by it honest enough, and I'm grateful to the Lord for it. Now, hush." Hurrying back to their tent.

Stabbing the knife into the ground between his feet, Woody wiped his hands in the grass. "How you figure the good Lord lets such a thing as this happen, Mack? Whole city shaking and burning down around us, and Him not lifting a finger to make it right."

Mack shrugged, saying, "Sent you the ham, didn't He?"

"Could be He lost a hand of poker with Old Scratch," Woody said, "and hell got set loose."

"Was thinking that very thing," Mack said, swirling the dregs around his coffee tin.

"Not a funning matter, Mack."

"Remember what Pearly told you about thinking them thoughts."

Sitting quiet a moment, Woody said, "Well, I ain't got a pocket to turn out like most of these poor souls, that's for sure, but I aim to be getting out of the pleasuring business. No offense to Pearly."

"And do what?"

"Don't know that part yet. Just know the time's come for me to light out. What say you, Mack? The Empress and Pearly's gone to ground, along with our ways of providing. Nothing to hold us in a city that's gone dead."

"Should've been somewhere yesterday," Mack said, getting up, tossing the dregs from the tin, glancing in the direction of Mabel's tent.

. . . JUMPING THE BREAKS

COMING AWAKE, finding himself on an army cot, Levi Hayes was slick with sweat, every inch of him hurting. He looked around the dingy hospital tent. Moving one foot, then the other, taking stock.

Light from outside sent shapes across the canvas walls. Rows of cots lined the interior, the injured tended by a handful of sisters. Smelling ether and alcohol, he flipped off the flimsy blanket, saw his cut foot had been cleaned and wrapped in gauze. Sitting on the edge, he thought he might black out again.

Reverend Thadeus, clean shaven and in better trim, turned from a table, smiling as he lifted a pitcher and filled a tin. Walking to Levi and extending it. "Good to see you back in the pink of condition, my boy."

"Not sure about any pink of condition, Reverend." Sipping the water, Levi asked how he got there.

"That was something, what you did yesterday," Thadeus

said, telling how the soldiers had found him and the man he was carrying, nodding over to a cot farther down the row.

"You say yesterday?"

Thadeus nodded.

Levi put weight on his legs, his head fuzzy. Muscles in his back and legs screamed, tadpoles shimmying across his vision. Sitting back down. "Saying it's what . . . Friday?"

"The one thing I'm sure about," Thadeus said, sitting next to him on the cot.

Downing the water, Levi sat a moment longer, said he best get underway, knowing if Quinn was alive he already had the money. He'd be waiting, wanting the gold, wanting Levi to come to him. Levi eased the gauze-wrapped foot into a moccasin, his thighs throbbing. Putting weight on both feet sent a knifing pain through his calves.

The reverend steadied him, said he best catch more rest.

"That'll have to wait. What I need's a gun."

"A good drink always steadies me." Thadeus guessing the nature of the need, saying, "Nothing gets solved by the gun, son."

"A knife, then."

Thadeus frowned.

"Fires still going?"

"Nothing to be done but let them burn out."

Levi took it slow, allowing the daggers of pain. Running a hand over his face, he felt his brows and a good deal of hair on his head had been singed away.

"What you did is the measure of a man," Thadeus said, steadying him. "Now take some reward in that and lie back easy and rest some." Knowing he wouldn't.

"Could use some more of that water." Levi staying on his feet, handing him the cup, shuffling over to Howard's cot.

Thadeus went to the table and poured, calling it Adam's ale, bringing the tin to him.

Howard lay sleeping a few cots down, his face as pale as the sheet covering him, both legs set in plaster.

"He going to be alright?" Levi asked.

"Chance of losing the left foot on account of infection, but the doc guesses he'll pull through either way."

Levi stepped closer, saying, "No doubt you're right about resting up, Reverend, but there's something I got to finish."

Thadeus nodded.

Walking over, shoving the tent flap aside, Levi stepped into the bustle out front of the ferry terminal, army and firemen and refugees, the smoke still cloaking a good part of the city to the south. He found himself next to Lieutenant Jinks, faintness in his head and the tadpoles swimming in front of his eyes, guessing he might be arrested. Deserting the rescuers.

"If I didn't say it already," Jinks said, looking at the man with no brows or lashes. "I thank you for yesterday." Extending his gloved hand, not handcuffs.

Shaking the hand, Levi glanced up at the clock tower, time stopped near quarter past five, guessing that's when the first shock hit, knocking out the clockworks.

A dispatcher marched up, handing the lieutenant a folded message. Uncapping his canteen, the man splashed water in his cupped hand and ran it across the back of his neck, waiting while his lieutenant read.

Waving Sergeant Booth over, Jinks showed him the dispatch, saying, "Get Cobb to fetch a blast box and as many crates of that dynamite as he thinks we'll need, and have him get a detail assembled."

"Sir?"

"Looks like we're going to blast some blue-blood mansions this day."

Booth reread the dispatch before handing it back, Jinks saying to Levi, "Fires jumped the breaks, and General Funston requires more fire lanes, else all of Nob Hill's likely to burn to hell."

Booth saluted, nodding for the dispatcher to follow, and hurried to assemble his squad.

"Even the nabobs won't be spared this day," Jinks said to Levi.

"You say mansions?"

"Ones up on the edge of Nob Hill." Jinks showed the dispatch. "Half-dozen'll need to go."

Florence Healey's address was second on the list. Smiling, Levi looked south across the smoldering city, forgetting the stabbing pain, saying he wished he was fit enough to volunteer.

"You've done your part," the lieutenant said, offering the older man his hand again. "City's indebted to you, sir." Asking his name.

Levi said his name, then, "You indebted enough to allow me a sidearm?"

Jinks looked at him. "Asking me for a gun?"

"In a no-questions-asked sort of way," Levi said, adding the one he had when the soldiers took Howard Sommers from him would do fine, guessing the old man wouldn't miss it.

. . . BREAKING CAMP

A STONEMASON knelt and chipped at a brick, steam rattling the lid of a cauldron over a fire pit. A queue of people waited on the private ladling soup, another dishing water from a wooden barrel astride the back of a wagon. A telegraph man in a shabby uniform bumped past Mack, calling through funneled hands for Union telegraphers, walking between the rows of tents.

Mack and Woody stopped before the last drab tent in the line. Clearing his throat, Mack kept his voice low, calling her Mrs. Porter, then waited.

The flap peeled back, and she was smiling at sight of them. Fresh-scrubbed, with her hair up, she ducked past the pole in a print dress, her feet bare.

"Morning, gents." Color was back in her cheeks, a shine to her hair. Leading them a few steps from the tent, she said Emma and the ladies were in much need of rest.

"You're looking fit, ma'am," Mack said, an understatement, lifting his eyes from her.

"Corporal Hegg was good enough to find something closer to my size," she said to Mack, putting a hand on his arm. "Nothing compared to what you did for me."

Liking the corporal less every time he heard his name, Mack said, "Must say Hegg's a better judge of fashion than yours truly. I'll give him that."

Smiling, Mabel said, "But he didn't risk his neck in the process." Looking down at her feet, "And so far he hasn't turned up any kind of footwear at all."

"Yeah, well, hard to come by, that's for sure."

The two of them smiling at each other.

"We just come by to say our so-longs," Woody said. "Mack and me's heading on, now that you're safe and all."

She nodded, her hand dropping from Mack's arm.

"Gonna catch the first thing smoking, ma'am," Woody said.

"Course if there's something else we can do . . ." Mack said.

"One thing: you can call me by my name," reminding him it was Mabel, then said to Woody, "Ma'am's what they'll call me soon enough."

"Yes, ma'am."

Mack asked after Emma.

"Army doctor said she was dehydrated, but guesses she's got the hard bark of her mother."

"Glad to hear it," Mack said, smiling back.

"And the good corporal arranged for cooking utensils and such, and brought by a basket of eggs. I'd be more than happy to fix you some."

"Had some boiled already, and a fine ham to boot, but thank you just the same, ma . . . Mabel," Woody said. "Shame, that ham would've done nicely with your eggs." Adding he gave it to a passing woman and child. "The two of them looking awful busted."

"Then I'm glad you did, Woody, and I thank you again for looking out for us."

"Got it from this fellow —"

"Don't think Mabel needs all the details about your ham, Woody." To Mabel: "So, you'll be heading off someplace?"

"Well, we've got land, a place Milton bought, called it Saddle Ridge, but there's no family out here." She paused, then said, "Milton's folks hail from New Haven. Dairy farmers, I'm told."

"You don't strike me the milking-cow type."

"Not sure about any of it yet, but I might surprise you, Mack."

"Bet you would at that."

The two of them smiling some more.

Woody saying he had milked cows, did it regular as a youngster. "First thing to know, tie that cow up good and right, then get your bucket steady 'tween your feet, hands warmed up, and get yourself a good grip on them teats —"

"That's good, Woody," Mack said.

"Corporal reports our apartment block's gone, with everything else around it," Mabel said. "Tells me there's another refugee camp the army's setting up just for women with infants over in Sausalito. Says he's being reassigned there and reckons it's the best place for us. For now, anyway."

Mack nodded. "Me and Woody'd be happy to get you to the docks. I mean, you being familiar with us, and not so much with Hegg . . ."

"You've done more than plenty, Mack. Plus, Hegg's gone

to arrange for a buckboard or cart. Sure he'll see us safely aboard." Then she asked about Mack's own plans.

"First off, going to find Levi and see how what's ours fared out."

She drew up and kissed his cheek, saying he was a good man.

Not nearly good enough, he thought, knowing this was it.

The girls of the Presbyterian Mission Choir filed past, the last in line with a hoisted bedroll suspended from a pole, the bedroll dragging along the ground.

"Look," Mabel called to the girl, "your bedding's dragging in the dirt."

The girl turned and smiled, saying, "What the heck's the difference, ma'am?"

Mack watched Mabel smile and call back, "You're right, no difference, no difference at all."

The girl smiled, too, and skipped a step, keeping up with the others.

. . . LIGHTNING GAP

CLAMPING HIS hands on her ankles, Sergeant Booth pressed with all his weight, keeping her down and from lashing with those feet. His cap was gone. This woman crazy strong. Struggling to keep his grip on the thrashing ankles, warning her again, giving her a one-two-three count.

Barnes and Perkins had her pinned by the arms, Florence Healey twisting her torso, her mouth showing teeth, trying to bite. All of them had felt her kicks; Perkins's forearm was bleeding from a crescent bite.

On a three-count, they hoisted, carrying her out across the lawn, stopping partway to readjust grips, Perkins catching her teeth a second time, the three of them hurrying her past her prize perennials, downslope to the iron gate.

Private Darby followed, arms loaded with whatever personal belongings he'd been able to grab from the armoire. Articles of clothing dropped off the pile, Darby not stopping to pick them up. Drawing an overflowing cart of valuables — Ming and Tang statuary, Chinese bronze, African jade — Hamish the Scotsman banged through the front door, hurrying after the soldiers.

Corporal Redding had a no-nonsense way about him, marching Van Doy ahead of his bayonet's point. Despite his size, Van Doy went through the door as passive as a lamb, head bandaged, one arm in a sling, the other raised. The widow's hysteria, then her falling armoire, had taken all fight from the man.

Lieutenant Jinks placed the last crate of dynamite and went out through the door ahead of Cobb, the man unrolling a wire coil, kicking a boot at Precious, the dog prancing around their feet, barking and snapping.

"Is your house next, soldier boy?" Florence shrieked at the sergeant, twisting to break free. "Come on, let's go and blow up your fucking house."

"I have my orders, Mrs. Healey." Tightening his grip on the ankles.

Shrieking at them, "I'm like *this* with E.E. Schmitz — the fucking mayor, in case you're an idiot." Twisting one finger over the other.

"Be as chummy as you like with the well-to-dos, ma'am, but even so, I've got orders to create fire lanes to save the rest of the city. And that's what I'm doing. The good mayor'd likely tell you the same if he were here."

Tipping her head back, she yelled for Van Doy. "Do something, you big stupid . . ."

Setting her down, the three soldiers held fast, Booth snapping restraints on her wrists, his boys holding fast on an ankle apiece. Van Doy, Hamish and her servants lined along the wall past the gate, looking on. Florence trying to kick. Neighbors from next door coming out, the elderly couple looking dignified, watching.

"Promise you, ma'am. I'll shackle you to your iron gate, you keep it up."

"Fuck off, you runt!" She was screaming, promising to find out where he lived and come burn his house to the fucking ground.

"Ball a gag in that mouth, Booth," Jinks said, glancing over at the neighbors, the old woman's jaw dropping open. Advising Florence, "Best duck your head now, ma'am." He nodded to Cobb. Cobb, the man well-versed in explosives and propellants, the man in charge of wiping Arch Rock from the Bay all those years ago, attached the wires to his wooden blast box. Then he started his count. On three, he jammed the plunger down, setting the charges, winking at Florence as he did so.

A slight delay, all heads ducking below the stonework. All but Florence, the woman watching, ten feet from the spot where she'd met the Aussie sailor just days ago. The front of the mansion, the architectural feat of San Francisco, exploded in an earsplitting shock of sound. The ground shook and fragments flew and dust rolled up like a curtain. Hadn't settled when the second and third blast left the structure gutted to its spiral staircase. Chunks of concrete toppled end over end, tearing up her fine lawn, ripping through the perennial beds.

As the cloud settled, Cobb picked up the blast box, tucked it under an arm, started for next door with the rest of the men, saying to her, "Army thanks you, ma'am, contributing this fine fire lane."

. . . WAYLAYING

WHAT REMAINED of the wood structures along Battery showed heavy damage, resembling matchstick hulls with tumbled walls, most of the roofs caved in, the street heaved in broken slabs of paving bricks. The St. Anthony's Mission had slid off its foundation, ending partway in the street. The wall the drunks that had sat against Monday morning had long scattered. Fires threatened from three blocks off, the breeze now helping it along Lombard.

Low resonance of distant explosions reached him, Levi guessing it was Jinks and his squad, painting a picture of the Healey place being laid to waste. That fine manor, nothing but a hole in the ground. It felt good.

"Here's to you, Florence Healey," he called out, the ship-yard's stack showing up ahead, the word *Healey* in bold letters.

In spite of his aches, he was grinning ear to ear, picturing the murderous bitch holding her yapping dog by her gate, helpless as Jinks blew up her place.

Hunched residents, some the employees of Healey Shipbuilding, watched him pass, hollow-eyed, their belongings piled out front of the desecrated rooming house. No activity inside the shipyard gates.

He walked on toward the House of Blazes, knowing this was the last time, set on the thirty thousand in coins, plastered behind the cellar wall. He'd get it . . . and be gone.

Thinking of Quinn Healey again, Levi checked the load, then tucked Howard Sommers' pistol in his belt. Jinks had told him back at the Depot he couldn't let a man have a weapon in times of martial law, nodding at Corporal Redding's pack along the wall, Howard Sommers' pistol in there for safekeeping, the noncommissioned man napping against the wall next to it. Jinks stepped away, tending to his squad.

Tongues of red started showing along Whiting now, stealing along the rooftops, feeding on the boarding houses, the wooden flops and dives. Favoring his cut foot, Levi picked up his pace, time not in his favor.

. . . FIRE LANES

THE BOOM rolled, the billow lifted on the razed mansion and torn grounds, the smell of gunpowder hanging in the air. Half the south wall of the carriage house remained. Jinks ordering his soldiers to pack up the wagon. Cobb had done his job, and they were moving next door.

Private Darby had drawn the short straw, having to escort Florence down to the docks, get her onboard with her hands manacled. Might have to slap on the leg irons if the crazy woman kept up the kicking. Booth and Redding were bellowing at another neighbor's door, announcing their purpose, calling for the inhabitants to step out and vacate the premises.

Darby turned his head to next door, the old couple standing in the road, looking up at their fine home about to be blown to rubble. That's when Florence kicked at him, then bolted through the gate, her hands fastened behind her.

"Hey!" If she wasn't a woman, he might have fired a shot. Attempting escape. Promising Van Doy and Hamish each a bullet if they so much as moved, he gave chase, yelling for Florence to halt. Running after her across the ragged lawn, dodging chunks of mansion.

Calling for Precious, Florence stumbled toward the ruin, no sign of the dog. Tears streaming down her face.

Darby tackled her to the ground, the woman twisting, fighting him with teeth and knees. Darby hauled her to her feet, holding her by the scruff, calling for the irons. Leading her back, he said, "Bite me again, you crazy . . . and . . ." He couldn't bring himself to say the words, shaking her instead, putting the meaning into it.

She spat at Darby, looked at the grinning Van Doy and Hamish. "You two fucks are fired. Never to work in this town again."

The two of them grinning, Hamish asking, "What town's that, ma'am?"

Looking up at her lawn, she looked once more for Precious. One of her maids stepping forward, Florence looking at the woman, didn't even know her name, the woman offering her kerchief, saying it would all be alright.

. . . ROLLING THUNDER

TRYING TO whistle hurt Levi's jaw, a souvenir from being slugged by Marvin Healey. The man had a ten-gallon fist and the size to lay behind it. Whistling was something from his boyhood years, something Pap taught him, something he'd never quite mastered. He whistled anyway, thinking, *let it hurt.* The roll of the distant explosions inspired the music in him. The Healeys were beaten — not by his own hand, but beaten just the same. The mansion had been blown to hell, and the shipyard was in line of the flames. Only a few blocks away.

His jailhouse sharpness had been dulled, and he didn't see Purvis lurking by the rooming house wall, in the shadows of the porch. Hawk leaned inside the opposite doorway of the place he'd just plundered, yanking a tobacco twist. Levi walked between them in the street, whistling and kicking a chunk of brick with his moccasin.

"Well now, Hawk, look who's come to call," Purvis said,

stepping off the porch, setting his pack down, the reservist's carbine coming off his shoulder and pointing at Levi.

Levi's hand went for Howard's pistol. Hawk dropped the twist, stepping out, drawing his pistol. Levi eased his hand away.

A Stanley Runabout, green with red wheels, laden with loot, chugged up from the top end of Battery. A scruffy drunk behind the wheel stopped and hopped out, a pair of Colts under a loose shirt, chains and necklaces around his neck. Hefting a bottle of Old Nick and cackling like a crone, he recognized Levi from out front of St. Anthony's. The auto packed high with cases of booze, foodstuffs and sacks of loot, rifle and shotgun barrels sticking out the back.

"Maybe this fella'd like that drink now, Cal," Purvis called to the driver, spewing tobacco juice at Levi's feet. Wiping his mouth, looking around the dead street, liking the way this day was turning out. His hand touched the lump still on his head. "I remember you, som'bitch."

Levi looked at him, waging his chances.

"Yeah, the one thinks interfering in a fellow's business is a righteous thing," Purvis said. "Going to drink with me now, ain't you? 'Fore you make your amens."

Stepping past the front of the auto, Cal held the bottle out to Levi, Levi ignoring it.

Taking it, Purvis tipped the bottle back, carbine hooked under the other arm. Hawk backed to the porch, picked up the twist, shoved it in his mouth, leaned on a beam, his pistol on Levi. Cal stood by the front of auto, letting Purvis put on a show. Setting the bottle and rifle down by his pack, Purvis stepped in. It was a solid punch that sent Levi sitting in the gravel, the three of them laughing.

"Not such a big man now," Purvis said, standing over him.

"Let's have a look at that pistol," Hawk said, nodding at Levi's belt, keeping his own gun trained on him.

Drunk or not, Hawk couldn't miss from this range. No way Levi would get a shot off. Easing out Howard's gun, he tossed it at Purvis's feet.

Lighting a cigar stub, Cal leaned against the Stanley's fender, balancing a fresh bottle on a headlamp. Purvis drew his skinning knife, looking down the blade, saying, "Got something to add to our poke?"

"Got nothing," Levi said, staying down, his fingers finding the chunk of brick he'd been kicking. "Lost what little I had."

"That's a plumb pity," Purvis said, stooping for Howard's pistol, looking at it. "Don't allow these past the Pearly Gates, case you ain't heard."

"Sure he ain't holding back now?" Hawk said around the cheek of tobacco, egging Purvis on.

"Wouldn't surprise me one fucking bit, Hawk." Purvis tried tucking the pistol in his belt. "Guess we'll know soon enough." The trigger caught his buckle, the gunshot blowing a hole through his trousers, his eyes round as dollars, thinking he'd killed himself, looking down to his feet.

Cal squawked at sight of the trousers blowing out, Hawk laughing like he was suffering convulsions, tobacco juice dribbling from his mouth.

"Think it's a laughing matter, som'bitch?" Purvis said, tossing aside Howard's pistol, coming at Levi with the knife, swinging it, too drunk to be fast.

Lashing out a foot, Levi slowed Purvis, his fist closing on the chunk of brick. Crabbing around so Hawk couldn't get a clear shot, Levi rolled as Purvis lunged with the knife, Levi kicking to keep him back, the blade slicing Levi's moccasin. Blade down, Purvis circled in a crouch, timing another lunge, hoping to afford Hawk a clear shot.

The shot ringing out had Levi thinking that was it, Hawk's scream cutting the air, Purvis wheeling, dropping the knife, going for the carbine.

Corkscrewing to the ground, Hawk clutched his leg, face in a grimace, blood and bone where his knee had been, the pistol dropping from his hand.

Purvis and Cal were firing up the street, Quinn Healey stepping out, the twin satchels slung over his shoulders. His useless arm hanging in a sling.

Using the wheel as cover, Cal knocked the bottle away from the fender, steadying the barrel and firing. Quinn's next shot struck the Stanley, Cal ducking down and scrambling down the side, wanting to get behind Quinn. From a crouch, Purvis lined his shot, Levi springing with the brick. Same time, Quinn turned and fired and put one square in Purvis's chest, knocking him into Levi, both going down in a tangle of limbs. Blood spraying from Purvis's mouth.

Holding the dying man in front, Levi snatched the skinning knife.

Reaching his pistol, Hawk got off a round from the ground. Quinn shot him as he came past the auto, Cal crawling around to the back of the auto. Stepping to Hawk, Quinn swept away the pistol, but the man was dead. He looked at Purvis, Levi hiding under him, then he turned.

Cal's next shot went wild, and he was up and diving into the Stanley, grabbing at the crank, trying to start it. The man screaming. Arm straight out, Quinn shot him, knocking him back, the body flopping across the passenger side, blood spattering the seat.

Stepping up easy, Quinn put in fresh cartridges, saying

to Levi, "I keep turning up and pulling you out of one pile of shit or another."

"Yeah, well . . ." Pushing Purvis off, Levi stayed down, the knife under his leg, piece of brick under his hand. "Suppose I could say thanks."

"Started thinking you weren't coming." Easing the satchels from his shoulder, Quinn stepped close, dropping in the last shell, snapping shut the cylinder, stepped on Levi's hand and cleared away the chunk of brick with his shoe. "Figured you must've got yourself killed."

"Thanks for caring." Levi shook the hand.

"Something I been burning to ask?"

"About the gold?"

Quinn grinned.

Levi sprang, one hand slapping at the pistol, the other burying the skinning knife to the bone.

Wailing, Quinn reeled back and yanked the trigger, firing into the dirt. Letting go of the pistol, he clutched his leg, growling in agony, dropping to the ground, his hands clutching either side of the blade sticking from his leg.

Sweeping away Quinn's pistol, Levi picked up Howard's, reached for the satchels, Quinn holding on to the straps, locking his jaws, half-growling, half-moaning.

Levi drew the blade from Quinn's thigh, waited for the scream to ease before saying, "That was for Red Tom." Tossing the knife away, he left the lawman to his howling, guessing he'd bleed out in the street, wanting it to be slow. He started up Battery, the fires moving this way, a little more than a block away now. Barely time to get down in the cellar and break out enough of the wall.

Mad with pain, moaning and growling, Quinn tried plugging the bleeding with his thumbs. Dragging himself over to Purvis, he ripped at the dead man's shirt, tearing a strip and tying a tourniquet, easing the bleeding, the dead man's revolver next to him. Grabbing it, cocking and lining it across Purvis's back, he squeezed off a shot.

Thirty yards off, Levi stumbled, dropping a satchel. Half-turning like he didn't believe it. Levi fired back, got behind a fence plastered with handbills declaring life was better with Anchor Steam Beer. Then he was gone.

. . . RIFTING

VERNA CULP eased herself onto the bale in back of the oxcart, the best thing on wheels Corporal Hegg could find, not sure if the smell was manure or something rotting. Mack helped Agnes up beside her, going to the side, taking Emma from Mabel long enough for her to step onto the seat, assisted by Hegg, Mack hiding his dislike for the man.

"It seems all you've done is look out for me since that day at the Mission," Mabel said, reaching for Emma.

"Were times you were looking out for me," Mack said, wiggling his finger, Emma's hand wrapped around it, kissing the baby's forehead.

Mack handed her up to Mabel. An awkward goodbye, Corporal Hegg clucking to the team, shaking the reins.

The cart rolled over the uneven ground, the wheels slipping in and out of the ruts. Mack watched till the wagon was at the edge of the encampment, abreast of the Presbyterian

Mission Choir's whitewashed sign, the girls lending voice to "Like a Rock in the Billows."

"We going?" Woody asked.

Mack turned for the tent, realized he had nothing to get, said, "Yeah, we're going."

. . . FIRE WITH FIRE

LIKE BLACK snow, the ash floated onto the deserted street. The House of Blazes looked about to fall in. Hiking up the satchel sent shooting pain through Levi's side. Every step was agony. Drawing his hand from his shirt, he looked at the blood, light in color, knowing what it meant. Steadying himself against the porch beam, he heard it coming.

The Stanley chugged up Battery, rubble in the street bucking Quinn on the seat. Clamping his teeth, he squeezed the tiller.

Levi ducked inside the House of Blazes.

Stopping out front, Quinn Healey dragged himself out, leaving the engine running, leaning and trying to use the carbine like a crutch, sticking the barrel in the dirt, the tourniquet soaked red, blood dripping down into his boot.

Leaving the satchel on the seat, Quinn took the pistol in his good hand, half-hopping for the door, agony in every move, a trail of bloody footprints behind him, getting through the doorway as fast as he could, not allowing Levi Hayes much of a target. Waiting, then moving along the wall, he let his eyes adjust to the gloom, ears sharp for any sound. Then over to the bar, barely missing the open trapdoor a second time. Past the bar, keeping low, he got to the workbench, leaning his weight against it, laying the carbine on the top.

Listening.

Little light spilled down the staircase, showing both lids on the casks.

Not the way he left them.

Raising the pistol, he took aim, saying, "Get the fuck out of there."

From the stack of crates, Levi came at Quinn's blindside, swinging Florence's sack of loot up from the floor, Quinn turning into it, struck in the face. The shot was deafening, pigeons flapping above him on the roof beams. His shot was wild, toppling him back onto the workbench. The pistol clattered from his good hand.

Dropping the sack, Levi jumped on him, shoved his own pistol barrel under Quinn's chin.

Quinn let his own pistol slip to the straw.

Levi waited through the pain, leaning into the man, saying, "Your lady's trinkets back," tilting his head at the sack. Nudging Quinn's revolver away with his foot, Levi pressed the muzzle of his own, saying, "Don't know where she'll put 'em. Army just blew her mansion to shit." Fighting the dizziness, his tongue feeling like cloth. If he felt the black come, he'd pull on the trigger. "Been thinking about this . . ." Levi nodded over at Red Tom, dead on the hay by the wall.

"On account of a dead Indian?" Leaning back on the workbench, Quinn measured his chances of overpowering Levi.

"That and the gold from the Mint."

"Really did it, huh?" Quinn grinned.

"Got it in tin cans, right down in the cellar." Levi nodded toward the trapdoor.

"Why you wanted that deed?" The spreading stain on Levi's shirt and the rasping breath told Quinn the man didn't have long. "Feels good telling me, getting it off your chest."

"Just letting you know how close you got." The pistol felt heavy, Levi lowering the barrel against the bleeding thigh, finger on the trigger, wanting to blow a hole big enough to drop a Barber dime through. Coughing blood, he knew he wouldn't be digging around in any cellar.

"How about we work a split?" Quinn said.

"How'd that work?"

"I'm not a greedy man. Just want a piece. Rest is yours. The cockfight money, too. You keep it."

"Already all mine."

"Ever drive one of them?" Quinn nodded at the window, the auto out front. "Me, I'll get you out of here." Leaning forward a bit, Quinn measured his chances, knowing Levi was fading, saying, "Still want, I'll throw in the deed."

"Gold's been down there the whole time," Levi said, nodding to the trapdoor. "Six years."

"Tore this place apart. Never found it."

"Believe what you want." Levi pressed the barrel.

"Shooting me, know what that gets you?"

"Feeling good." Levi's breath came in shallow jags. Reaching, he shook the cuffs from Quinn's belt, snapping an end on the broken wrist, Quinn wincing.

Levi jerked on the cuffs, Quinn crying out. Snapping the free end to the bench leg's brace, he fished through Quinn's pockets, then tossed the keys toward the stairs, waiting through a bolt of pain.

Quinn made his move then, trying to strike with his elbow. Levi pulling the trigger as he was knocked back. Howling, Quinn dropped, his broken wrist held up by the cuffs. The shot had missed the leg and gone through his foot.

Down on the straw floor, Levi saw the fire dancing out front, lay there till the front window shattered, flames licking up the interior wall.

Nobody was getting the gold. Levi realized it, and Red Tom was getting the burial he wanted.

Quinn pushed himself back up on the bench, far as the cuffs allowed.

"Tossed your fuck of a brother in the Bay." Catching the satchel strap, Levi forced himself to his knees, then up to his feet, saying, "Was your sweet Florence killed him."

Quinn grinned, not buying it. Watching the flames on their way to the ceiling.

"Yeah, it's so. Shot him in his ear. Did it two times."

Quinn twisted at the cuff, the fire spreading across the front wall.

"Caught her getting poled by two of Pearly's finest. Fuck of a brother didn't like that only one of them boys was white."

Quinn saying it was bullshit, tugging at the cuffs, crying out.

"Woman's sure got her share of traffic going in and out of those legs."

The fire rose to the top of the wall, feeding on the dry boards, getting as hot as a furnace in there.

"Ask Marvin yourself when you see him." The satchel was too much to lift, Levi leaving it, taking the skinning knife, moving back to Quinn.

Flames licked across the ceiling, the interior lit like in

old times, back when Hell Broke Lucy swung from the Spanish chandelier. Tossing the blade on the bench, Levi said, "A trapped animal'll chew off its leg to get free." Then he turned for the door, throwing an arm over his nose and mouth, walking through the wall of flames.

Taking the blade, choking on the smoke, Quinn went to throw it — couldn't miss from here. But where would that leave him? The carbine was out of reach, the keys over by the stairs. Looking at the satchel, then to the door. Levi was gone.

Flames lapped at the clapboard, the crackling making it sound hungry, feeling red-hot against his skin. Levi lifting himself onto the Stanley's seat. The second satchel, on the passenger floor, made him smile, Cal dead and sprawled across, his head hanging out the far side, a mess of blood across the seat.

Quinn coughed, trying to yell from amid the snapping clapboard and groaning timbers. Smoke rolled from the door, the window breaking, fire jumping out.

The engine was still running, Levi looking at the controls. Never been in a motor car before. Blundering at what to do, he ground the stick into gear, the Stanley lurching forward.

●

HOT ENOUGH to peel skin. Quinn jerked at the cuffs. The rocket of pain shot up his arm, nothing against the terror of being burned alive. Flames spread and curled at the ceiling beams. A board clattered down, then another, sparks flying back up to the roof beams. Hot as an incinerator.

Glimmers and shadows danced like demons, smoke choking and billowing. Couldn't quash the panic, Quinn swatting at sparks. A deep breath and a gathered rush, he let go a yell, lugging the bench straight at the door, the wooden legs sliding on the scattered hay. Throwing his weight, he heaved the bench at the opening. Levi sitting out in the Stanley, watching him.

Flinders flew and wood struck the doorway, the frame splintered down one side. Gulping hot air, Quinn shoved the bench back, hay catching all around his feet. Rushing again, the frame ripping free the second time. Couldn't feel the broken hand or the foot at all now.

Backing the bench farther into the oven, Quinn thought one more charge would do it.

The upper floor was totally aflame now.

Eyes on the freedom beyond the doorway, Quinn dropped his weight low and dragged the bench for the opening.

A joist crashed down, the floor shaking, turning to a sea of fire. Part of the staircase crashed down onto the bar, tumbling off, the roof groaning above him, the upper floor sagging.

The bench was cracked, a leg knocked loose, but time was running out, Quinn stomping at the flames, his trousers catching.

Rushing for the last time, he screamed, his bloodied foot hooking on the trapdoor; Quinn pitched down into the open cellar, like falling through a gallows, dropping as far as the cuffs allowed, dangling and screaming, the roof caving in above him. The gold somewhere below him.

. . . RUNABOUT

MAKESHIFT KITCHENS lined the street, temporary and abandoned, kindling stacked next to a stove of piled bricks. Mack and Woody moving through the apocalypse, the House of Blazes a few streets west. Both kept watch, Mack looking to the left side, Woody the right, no desire to be mistaken for looters.

A white-haired woman sat atop a trunk on a knocked-out curbstone as if she were waiting on a trolley. Mack called to her. The makings of a cigarette in her hand. She eyed them, not saying a word, tongue licking the paper.

An alleyway between buildings on the Bay side allowed a glimpse of the rescue boats. A ferry, the name *Eureka* across its wheelhouse, sounded and steamed for the Oakland side, Mack thinking of Mabel and the child, thinking they could be onboard.

"Don't think we ought to go another step," Woody said,

seeing the rising smoke ahead, his eyes darting around. "Heard the fire chief was the first one smited by the evil hand."

"Uh huh." Mack kept walking.

"And all before the fire ever got going. Same hand that turned off all the water, hand of old Satan." Woody looked back at the old woman, hurried his steps, keeping up to Mack. "You hearing me?"

"Remember what Pearly told you," Mack said, the crackling in the distance telling him they weren't going much farther. "It gets too bad, we'll just turn around."

"That up ahead's faster than us, Mack."

"Yeah, but we'll be alright."

"Chinatown got swiped clear like a checkerboard, just like that. Faster than all them living down there." Woody repeating what the telegraph man had said at the camp. "We the only ones ain't got sense enough to go in the right direction."

"We're just having a look, staying to the middle of the street. Said we'll be alright. Now —"

"And with General Funston decreeing the martial law, yes sir, we'll be in for it. Soldier boys shooting folks right in the street."

Mack put up a hand to slow him down.

"And with me not near as white as you or this E.E. Schmitz."

"Alright. You turn back if you want, take the old woman with you, she's white, but I'm going to find Levi."

Turning again, Woody looked at the old woman still watching, blowing a cloud of smoke, Woody saying, "I've done some thinking, Mack . . . you and me . . ."

"Yeah?"

"Best be heading out west, away from this devil's town."

"Out west, huh?" Mack figured Woody was too spooked to get the geographical unfeasibility.

"Uh huh, someplace like Texas."

A sign hung on a support in front of the Golden City Cafe, its wall caved away: *Gone to hell, back in six months*, Mack thinking he just ate the daily special a week back, something with a French name that cost two bucks.

The next block, the smell and sound of the fire grew. Sprawled bodies of the men Quinn gunned down lay in the street, Mack recognizing the two drunks from out front of the Mission.

"Like that army fellow told us, his boys are out here shooting anything looks like a looter," Woody said, eyeing the dead and their packs on the ground. "These gents being looters and that being their booty."

"We're no looters, and we got no loot."

"These fellas might've said the same."

The Healey berths and gantry showed above the tin roof past the junction at Telegraph. A sand-haired boy with a wooden wagon filled with belongings stood peering into a wide fissure that ran up the middle of the street in a jagged rip. The rail track had split in two, the ties looking like broken teeth, the rails twisted. Water from a broken main filled the gap, turning it into a pool.

Mack asked the boy where his folks were, getting a shrug for reply. The boy looking at Woody, who was gushing tears, the dead in the street causing him to think of Pearly again.

"Never mind him," Mack said, pointing the boy in the direction of the Depot; told him take the old woman with him. The boy saying, "Do it for a dollar, sir."

Mack told him to just get on and do it, the boy shrugging

and hauling his wagon by the handle, starting off, the wheels bumping over the rough ground.

The topmast of a tall-sail ship showed between two three-story buildings, out past the docks, gliding out across the Bay, same direction the ferry had taken, the crow's nest disappearing in the low ceiling of smoke rolling out from ahead of them, refugees crowding against the rail. Too far out to distinguish faces.

Fire blocked their path at Telegraph, flames feasting on the dilapidated structures along Battery. A motor car stood in the middle of the street, a figure slumped across the tiller. As far as he was going.

"Good Lord's sent us a sign, left that so's we can ride out of here," Woody said.

Mack took a couple more steps, then stopped, recognizing the figure. "Levi!" Mack rushed to him, easing Levi's head back, his shirt blood-soaked.

Opening his eyes, Levi winced, saying, "What the fuck took you?"

"Too long a tale to tell," Mack said, unbuttoning Levi's stained shirt, the satchel on the seat that looked like someone had butchered meat on it.

Levi turned his head toward the Healey Shipbuilding empire catching fire. "Glorious sight, huh?"

"Sure is," Mack said, checking the wound. "Guess you met up with the other Healey."

"Had some words."

Mack peeled off his own shirt. Gently as he could, he pressed it to the exit hole in Levi's chest, his uncle losing a lot of blood.

Levi clutched at the seat, the pain racking through him.

"This contraption work?" Mack asked, looking at the

controls. On the running board, he leaned across Levi, pressing on the shifter. The Runabout lurched and stalled, Levi slumping forward, Mack catching him from falling. No idea how to get it started again, and no time for finding out.

. . . SOARING

THE FLOTILLA, composed of anything able to cross the Bay, waited to dock, only two piers fit for use. Refugees by the hundreds still pressed forward under the protection of the fireboats' geysers, the crews continuing to soak anything that could burn. Rainbows showed in the mist they created.

Mack pulled Levi along in the sand-haired boy's wagon, going as fast as he dared, the wooden wheels clanking on the cobblestone. Kicking a clod out of the wagon's path, he kept looking back at him, Levi slumped and facing backwards in the wagon, drifting in and out, muttering things that made no sense, his head swaying, feet dragging. He tried telling Mack where to dig, the back wall at the floor, back in the old coal room. Every now and then Levi jerked, like he feared he was falling.

Walking alongside, Woody kept a hand on Levi's shoulder, doing his best to steady him, describing the taste of glazed ham to the boy, who had never had it. Exaggerating

how big the one he'd had was, Woody promised he'd find
the boy something fitting to eat down by the terminal. The
boy walking along, holding his hand, holding on to the old
woman with the other, the woman not in her right mind,
just walking along, bowlegged and all stooped over, smoking
and not talking.

The satchel between his knees, Levi winced as one of the
wagon wheels hopped over another clod. He came around,
opening his eyes, saying, "Jesus, Mack, think you missed
one." Coughing more blood.

"This look like a proper ambulance wagon to you?"
Mack said, looking back at him, sorry as hell he hadn't seen
that one.

"Reminds me of a time . . ." Levi couldn't finish.

"Of when I was a youngster, and you pulling me in a
wagon?"

Levi tried to smile.

"Anybody ever tell you talk too much?" Mack asked, glad
Levi hadn't asked about Pearly yet, Mack hoping Woody
wouldn't start up about it. He'd have to find a way to tell him
later. Hoping there was a later.

Levi reached in the satchel, fumbling and shoving a
stack of bills at Woody.

"What's that?"

"Fuck's it look like?" Mack said, Levi waggling his hand
for Woody to take it.

"What am I gonna . . ." Woody stared at it in his own
hands.

"Wants you to get yourself that new beginning you been
going on about," said Mack.

Woody was speechless for once, gawking at the money
in his hands. More than he'd ever seen in one place, feeling

like somebody who had just been elevated to the rank of the affluent.

"Where's your widow?" Levi tried to say, not able to turn and look at Mack.

"Got them safely on the Sausalito ferry."

"Put her there personal, huh?" Levi said, grinning and coughing.

"Have your fun, old man," Mack said, feeling the weight of blame for not staying with him.

Levi tried to say it was damn Christian of him, but the words wouldn't come.

"The woman had a child, case you didn't notice," Mack said, wishing he could hurry the wagon along East Street, a cool breeze coming off the Bay now. "Poor woman all alone in this godless place, without so much as her man to give a damn for her and that child."

"Heard what I said . . . about where to dig."

"Yeah, I heard it."

"Burned to the ground or not, it'll be there," Levi said. "Want you to —"

"Worry on that later."

The columns of the ferry station showed in the distance, Mack pulling the wagon around the broken road. Looked like a pair of Jinks's soldiers out front by the hospital tent, big red cross on it.

Levi sank in the wagon, his feet scuffling along the ground. Felt he was floating over the American River again, felt himself topping a bluff. Woody helped to prop him up.

"That sums to a life of hardship," Mack went on, trying to keep Levi conscious, pulling the wagon easy over more rough ground.

Coughing, Levi was seeing the sawmill beyond the tips

278

of the dogwoods, Pap panning in the tailrace, waving to him, calling his name.

"Woody, run up ahead and fetch the sawbones." Mack said.

"Where am I gonna find —"

Mack's look stopped him, Woody tucking the money into his shirt, leaning Levi gently forward, then taking off.

"Handsome widow woman," Levi tried to say, coughing, reaching back in the satchel, his breathing more ragged. Drifting in and out — him and Pap dancing in the stream, placer gold gleaming in a pan. Felt the icy water on his skin again.

"Glad you're enjoying yourself, old man," Mack said, watching Woody run to the soldiers, the man flapping his arms like he might take flight.

Levi dug in the satchel and pressed more bills into the sand-headed boy's hand.

The boy didn't understand.

"Wants you to get yourself a better wagon, son," Mack said.

Nodding, the boy tucked the bills into a pocket, thanking him. Holding the old woman's hand, the boy walked on to the Depot, hoping the black man would hold true and get him some of that ham.

Mack stopped and let go of the handle, same time Woody reached the soldiers, his arms still flapping. Mack knelt and propped Levi's head, the tears coming.

Drawing a ragged breath, Levi felt the pain leave him. Then he was floating over the American River again, topping that bluff, the sawmill beyond the tips of the dogwoods, an old man and boy panning in the tailrace, the two of them dancing and splashing in the stream.

ACKNOWLEDGMENTS

As ALWAYS, it's been a pleasure working with Jack David and everybody at ECW Press — what an amazing team. A big thank you to my editor, the talented Emily Schultz. I'd also like to thank my copy editor, Peter Norman, who catches everything, and David Gee for a fourth great cover design. And to Xander, the best son in the world, for his friendship and support in all my creative endeavors.